Tamzin has found some answers to her strange and complicated life. Confronting her parents, the architects of her problems, was never going to be easy, but she has finally cornered them in a cafe. The answers, when they come, are shocking, but Tamzin can now move on with her life, marry Matin Campania, and work with him on a new and challenging venture.

Meanwhile, Nelis Winter and Xavier Partridge are also getting married after a year of romance and planning. Things are going their way, but they can't give their friend Lucy an answer to the question of what happened to her cousin Dequan's first girlfriend who vanished back in 2009. Nelis makes a wish to help Lucy with her puzzle, but she has no idea if it will work. Anyway, her own future is more enticing than trying to solve a decade-old mystery.

Tamzin, now in possession of her old memories and happily married to the love of her life, has let go of her obsession with Dequan, but Matin is convinced she will meet him again and make a belated explanation for her abrupt disappearance from his life.

Tamzin can't see how this will ever happen, but her life is already stranger than any fairy tale, and in the end she accepts that Matin is usually right. She leaves the matter in the lap of fate, but fate hasn't finished its games with Tamzin yet!

Being Tamzin 7
Copyright © 2022 Lark Westerly
ISBN: 978-1-4874-3429-8
Cover art by Martine Jardin

Published by eXtasy Books Inc

Look for us online at:
www.eXtasybooks.com

Being Tamzin 7

By

Lark Westerly

DEDICATION

For Tina, Jay, Cat and Bri . . . the mighty women who helped me to bring Being Tamzin to life.

AUTHOR'S NOTE

The *Fairy in the Bed* series features a sprawling cast of characters who wander in and out of one another's stories. For more about this series, visit Lark's website at https://larksinger.weebly.com

The seven volumes of *Being Tamzin* tell Tamzin's story, but some of the other characters will be familiar via the following books.

Dequan Qin first appeared in *Queen of the May,* and his romance is told in *Geese a Laying,* and *Just Eloped.*

Lucy Tan first appeared in *The Pear Tree.* She fell in love with Paris in *Queen of the May.*

Nelis Winter and Xavier Partridge got together in *The Pear Tree,* which is also where Nelis met Frances and Niall.

Flick Dark has appeared in a few books. She met her husband in *Tied up in Tinsel.*

Tamzin appeared in a tiny part in the *Counterpoint* books, and also cameos in the *Queen of Tarts* books along with *Courtesan.*

Otto, who assisted in Rochelle's escape, met Nelis in *The Pear Tree,* and he encountered Lucy and Dequan in *Queen of the May.*

Like *Geese a Laying, Queen of the May,* and *Just Eloped, Being Tamzin* is partly set in 2020 and 2021. When I wrote *QotM,* Covid19 wasn't even thought of. By the time it was published, we were in the middle of a pandemic. Since it was far too late to rewrite the story, I had to let it be. That decision in turn affected the other books in this timeline. My philosophy is that as the world of *Fairy in the Bed* is not *quite* our world, we can accept that in that reality the pandemic didn't happen in 2020. In any case, it *can't* be our world, because Sydney trains don't allow non-assistance dogs as passengers.

Is this the end of Tamzin's story? Not exactly. She is likely to pop up at music festivals, including those held on Delphinium Island. Annie Blue and Kate Maple may yet get their own stories, and obviously Tamzin would be involved in those. Also — what exactly did Maggie Bróga-damhsa, Eamon the Red's lovie, mean when she spoke of bottled ban-sidhe in the cellar at Bellflower Cottage? Will the tiny dancing lady Tamzin remembers ever be identified? What about the kaleidoscope? Time will tell. Finally, for anyone interested in Takk Engel and her wee dog Puffin, there is a free short story involving her and the Dames with Dogs on the Being Tamzin website. She also appears in *One Hundred Roses*.

TIMELINE

Being Tamzin 1- 2009-2013

The Pear Tree — 2011 and 2019 Nelis and Xavier — Begins during Being Tamzin 1 and ends at the beginning of Being Tamzin 6

Queen of the May — 2011- 2020 Lucy and Paris Begins during Being Tamzin 1 and continues during Being Tamzin 7
Being Tamzin 2 — 2013 — 2017
Being Tamzin 3 — July 2017 — late November 2018
Being Tamzin 4 — Late November 2018 — March 2nd, 2019
Being Tamzin 5-July 2019 — December 2019
Being Tamzin 6 — December 2019 — March 2020
Being Tamzin 7-March 2020- April 2021

Geese a Laying — 2020 Dequan and Martina during Being Tamzin 7

Just Eloped — December 2020 Martina's nieces, Chiara and Lili, and Yannick — during Being Tamzin 7
Queen of Tarts trilogy — 2020-late 2021, finishing after Being Tamzin 7

One Hundred Roses — 2021-2022

PART ONE: TAMZIN

CHAPTER ONE: CREAM CAKE

Tamzin Herrick, Adelaide, March 1st, 2020

Tamzin Herrick had waited a long time to confront her parents. She'd run away from them the year she should have turned eighteen, and she'd had no contact with them since.

That was what she'd believed until today, anyway. Now she'd discovered that Ada and Mister Sinister, or whatever their names really were, were still playing their peculiar mind games with her and with everyone else.

They'd made her childhood a confusion of change and uncertainty. They'd forced her away from her first best friend, Emily, and they'd made her break up with her first love, Dequan, without a chance to explain or to say goodbye. They'd changed her name and her age and her possessions repeatedly, and they'd filled her with apprehensions.

And why?

For a *game*?

Maybe if she hadn't spent seven years in fairyland after she'd fled, she might have found out sooner. She might even have known, by now, whether this day in March really was her twenty-eighth birthday.

Apprehension was not a good companion, but now all those apprehensions had gone. She had her parents cornered in a coffee shop, and she felt solidly determined and utterly confident.

After all, Matin Campania was with her, and her darling elf man had promised her that her parents *would* explain themselves, whether they wanted to or not. Matin didn't break his promises.

She was aware of a lot of fuss from people behind them near Gallery Twenty-Five, but she was focused on *Galleria Coffee*—and on her cornered but oblivious quarry.

"We'll order something first," she whispered as they entered.

Matin turned his face to the counter, and after a sweeping glance behind them, he ordered a pot of tea for four, and four plates of cream cake.

"We're joining my fiancée's parents over at table nine," he said. He added, smiling, "We're determined to break down their resistance."

"Our cream cake will do that," the server said with a grin. "I'll bring it over. Cash or card?"

"Card." Matin took his wallet out of his pocket. "You go ahead, sweetheart. I'll be with you in a minute."

Tamzin blew him a kiss.

With a swish of her green dress and a determined tapping of her spy-heeled shoes, she walked over to table nine and pulled up a chair.

"Hi, Mum. Hi Dad . . . or is it still Breezy and Clem? How the hell are you?" She stared into their shocked faces, daring them to make a public scene. Then she said, quietly, "Penguin? Why does he call you *Penguin*?"

Her mother shrugged. "An Adelie is a kind of penguin. Hence—penguin. Paul always did have an allusive way with words."

"Paul and Adelie—what?"

"Who are Paul and Adelie? Our names are Ayesha and Joe Chaucer." Her mother tapped her chest. She wore a sports watch on her left wrist, and a plain gold wedding band. Her face was bare of makeup and her straight strawberry blonde hair was pinned up to fit in under a helmet.

2

She had lines in the corners of her eyes and a pair of bike gloves tucked in her top pocket.

Tamzin took in the stranger who had borne her in a glance, but she stuck to the matter in hand. "Your names are not Ayesha and Joe anything. Paul and Adelie—what?" She looked up as Matin slid into the seat beside her. "They're being obstructive."

He nodded to them. "Fou wasn't much hurt when you threw your bike at him," he said to Paul.

"That was—unfortunate. Spur of the moment reaction." He rolled his eyes to Adelie. "I *said* he should have been put down—but no, you had to play that last hand, right? You never did know when to fold."

"Don't you *dare* talk about Fou like that," Tamzin snapped. She added, "What happened to Barney? Did you put *him* down when he became an inconvenience?"

Adelie put out her hand as if to touch Tamzin's. Tamzin jerked away. Her gemstone bracelet, a birthday present from Matin, spat rainbow fire.

Adelie looked taken aback, but then she recovered. "No, of course we didn't put him down. Barney was my childhood dog. He lived to be fifteen. When he died, we got him a peace lily."

"You missed him when he went. You kept on asking for Ba-ba," Paul said.

"You left the peace lily behind."

He shrugged. "We couldn't take it on the ship. Quarantine laws. They don't live that long, anyhow."

"What?" Tamzin gave him a hard stare.

He shrugged. "Three years . . . five, tops."

"Well, that's longer than *I* got, the first time I was Tamzin."

Out of the corner of her eye, she saw Adelie's brows rise and Matin gave a tiny *humph* which presumably covered a desire to laugh.

"So, the lily in Room One's a fake?"

"Of course not. It's a living, breathing specimen of Spathi-phyllum *wallisii*." Adele sounded insulted.

Paul gave her an amused look. "Plants don't breathe, Mills. You ought to know that. Didn't you once work in a florist's shop?"

Adelie said, "It's a different specimen, but as close as we could get to the original."

The server came to the table and put down a loaded tray. "Enjoy," she said as she briskly removed items onto the table. She looked down, nonplussed, at the barely touched coffee Paul and Adelie had.

"I do hope you haven't added a purgative to that teapot, Alexandra," Paul said.

"Of course she hasn't, Joe. She'd never do that. It would affect them as well."

From dogs to peace lilies to things in coffee — Tamzin had almost forgotten how impossible conversations with her parents could be.

As if I'd put anything in their coffee . . .

She remembered her friend Daylight had put poteen in *hers* once, and she'd all but accused Daylight's friend Garret of adding something to the coffee when she'd been at *Wildwood Studio*.

That was different.

Tamzin struck the table with her fist, making the china clatter. "Will you two drop the act?"

Adelie said, "We Chaucers are twinned at the hip. A double act comes naturally."

"Forget the Chaucers. In fact, forget them all. I want your real names. Your original names. Your complete names. Paul and Adelie *what*?"

They stared at her, with the café lights reflecting in the biking Lycra.

Tamzin said, "I want *my* original name, in full. I know I

4

was called Alexandra — Zandie — "

"God no! Zandie is what *she* called you, against our express — "

Paul stopped Adelie with a tap on the wrist. His long ponytail was streaked with grey, and he had a mole high on one cheek. She didn't remember that, so it must be fake. He wore a black and white skull ring on his little finger. "Settle down, Penguin. Water under the bridge."

"Names," Tamzin said, implacably.

"All right. You made your point. Mind you, could have knocked us down with a feather when we found you'd reverted to Tamzin Herrick. Why did you do that?"

"Because I wanted to. Names. Otherwise, I will make a terribly public scene, and something will happen that you won't enjoy."

They sighed in unison. Then Paul said, "Paul Bysshe-Minister and Adelie Jane Spenser at your service — though it's hardly relevant. We haven't used those names for a long, *long* time. Twenty-five years, to be precise."

Bysshe-Minister — Sinister.

"Branok St Ives was right," Tamzin said to Matin. "He *said* maybe the original name was something that rhymed with *sinister*. Winchester, he thought. And Bysshe . . ."

"Some connection with Percy Bysshe Shelley's grandfather, or so my father said. Terribly tenuous, but then, he was terribly pretentious," Paul said.

"And Spenser — as in Gallery Spenser or Edmund Spenser, the Faerie Queen man?"

"Yes, that's right." Adelie leaned forwards. "To the literary wits that hung around Paul, that made *me* Fairy Penguin. I was practically forced to ring the changes."

"You should have married me when you got the chance, Penguin," Paul said.

"And become Penguin Bysshe-Minister? I don't think so!"

Tamzin hit the table again.

Her father looked at her reproachfully. "You were always a bad-tempered child. I see you're no better as an adult. How old are you now?"

"Twenty-eight today," Tamzin said through her teeth.

"God, are you really?"

She shrugged. "I chose to use the birthdate you assigned me as Tamzin. Do you even remember my real one?"

"Not for certain," Adelie said. "It was all a bit of a daze in those days. Could have been late New Year's Eve or early New Year's Day."

"Day. There were fireworks already starting while you were still yelling," Paul said.

"I'll take your word for it. *You* try having horrendous cramps in a taxi. The taxi driver wasn't much help."

"I was born in a *taxi*?" For some reason, Tamzin felt outraged by that. It seemed so — so impermanent.

"Yes. We had a few beers later to wet your head, and bonded."

"Bad idea," Adelie said.

Tamzin reflected that if she hit the table again, her fist would get sore. "What year was that?"

"Nineteen-ninety-three. Just."

"So, I'm still twenty-seven." She glanced at Matin. "But I'm keeping my gorgeous birthday present."

"Twenty-seven." Paul Bysshe-Minister reached for a plate of cake and cut off a piece with the edge of a teaspoon.

Tamzin poured herself some tea.

"Tea, Miss Spenser?" Matin asked belatedly of Tamzin's mother.

Bysshe-Minister shook his head. "The Chaucers are flat white drinkers when they drink coffee at all. Usually, it's hot water with a twist of lemon. Never *tea*. Who are you again?"

"This is Matin Campania. My betrothed."

"Come again?"

"We're engaged."

Adelie glanced at Tamzin's left hand.

She waggled her right one. "Over here, *Penguin*."

"Oh *God*," Adelie said. "You've found a fricking fairy."

"I have. In fact, I found several, but I get to keep the best one."

"I suppose that accounts for the get-up you're wearing."

"This is the dress I got for my formal . . . the one *you* were supposed to take me shopping for."

"Was I?"

"Yes!" she snarled. "You promised, but you didn't come home in time, so I had to go on my own."

"Water under the bridge," Bysshe-Minister said.

"Say that again and you'll wear that cake all over your fake ponytail," Tamzin spat.

Paul Bysshe-Minister grasped his tail of hair and tugged. "Nothing fake about this, my girl. I grew it, and the colour is natural. Might go for a man bun soon."

"Well, you obviously got to go to your formal, because I remember you sloping home from it looking like a wet week," Adelie said.

"Yes. You and Shades dragged me away the next day!"

"You got to finish the school year. How do you come to have that dress still, anyway?"

Tamzin breathed in sharply. "I hid it in that suitcase you forced on me." She held up her hands. "Enough!"

It was time to stop sniping and to get some answers.

"I want you to tell me exactly what you were up to, and how it ties in with the exhibition in there," she said, jerking her head towards Gallery Spenser.

"Well—"

"Do not begin with *well*. That indicates prevarication. Also, I want *one* of you to tell me. This double act is getting old.

How about I ask questions and you give me straight answers. After that, we'll leave, and you never need to see me again. You can play whatever games you want."

"Don't be like—"

For the third time, Tamzin hit the table.

She pointed at Adelie. "Number one, what do you want me to do about Fou? Do you want him back?"

Ada said, "No. He doesn't fit in with the Chaucer lifestyle. You can keep him."

Paul muttered, "Aside from the bike incident, which was an honest accident, we treated him well enough."

"You abandoned him."

"We gave him to our daughter to mind. How is that abandonment?"

Tamzin gritted her teeth. "Right. Now, how much of what you two said in Room One was true?"

"Most of it," Adelie said.

"How is Shades—Wayne Ellington—mixed up in this?"

"That's more difficult. We met him back when we first got together."

"At a costume ball," Paul said.

"You were Percy Shelley, and I was Mary with a bracelet of bolts in case you turned into Frankenstein's monster."

"That made no sense at all. I *told* you—"

"What is he?" Tamzin cut in.

"He went as a sinister magician, complete with white gloves, a wand and a rabbit," Adelie said.

Tamzin growled, "What *is* he?"

"Oh. He's a fixer. A facilitator. He helped us with a few matters."

"When did you find out he wasn't human?"

Adelie shrugged. "He is, partly. I think."

"But partly not."

"I guess we discovered it when we'd all had a bit much to

drink, and he showed us a few tricks that went beyond fishing a twenty-cent piece out of my ear. Paul is pretty good at sleight of hand—always has been—but the things himself could do went well beyond that."

So, Sinister Magician *isn't too far from the truth.*

"How did he come to be mixed up with all your life changes?"

"He—"

"Facilitated," Paul said.

"Why?"

For the first time, her parents looked disconcerted.

"Why what?" Paul asked.

"Why did he do it? Why did *you* do it—any of it? I ran through all sorts of ideas—witness protection, kidnapping, spies . . . criminal gangs . . . but none of them quite fitted. It took me a long time to work out why they didn't fit, but I finally did."

"Oh?" Adelie leaned forward again.

"You were enjoying it. And I thought if you'd really been afraid, as all that secrecy implied, you wouldn't have. But why did you start?"

"Money," Adelie said.

"Adventure," Paul corrected.

"Both."

Paul added, "We'd got into a bit of bother with my pretentious family, and Wayne suggested we might want to disappear for a bit. We talked it over and the idea grew from there. One of us—I forget which—proposed a change of identity. We didn't know if it would work. Just moving to another state didn't seem a good option. We'd be bound to run into someone who knew us, especially me, because I travelled with the firm."

"And got your face in glossy magazines," Adelie put in.

Paul continued, "For it to work, we'd have to *be* other

people. We'd both done a bit of *am Dram,* and role playing appealed to us. When you were born, we put the idea on the back burner, but then Wayne conceived the idea of making it pay for itself. He'd applied for a huge arts grant—and he got it."

"Living expenses for *twenty-five years,*" Adelie said. "So, we were off and running. I went to art school to make me a viable partner in the enterprise, and Wayne found us a nanny—off the books—to take care of you while we prepared the ground.

"We should have known better than to take his recommendation. We did, though."

"Nanny Lu," Tamzin said.

"You remember her?"

"No. But I know the name."

"She seemed perfect—wanted a place to live for a while, was happy to work for board, and she said she'd looked after a lot of younger siblings. You took to her. She used to take you out, and sometimes you'd be gone the whole day, and you'd come back wet and sandy. We assumed you'd been down on the beach, but then one day she took you out when I was supposed to take you shopping for shoes. We went down to the beach to find you. We saw you both going into a little cave . . ."

"You didn't come out. I went in after you and found a dead end," Paul said.

Adelie said, "We were worried *sick!* We called Wayne, and *he* told us to simmer down, that you were safe, and that he'd have a word with Lu and drag her into line."

"That's when we found out we'd hired a blooming fairy—Wayne's daughter," Paul said. "We didn't even know he had one. He'd knocked up some elf woman one Christmas. Lu was the result.

"We sacked her, of course, but she used to come in and—er—borrow you. Then one day she brought you back and you were screaming. You'd been hurt — cracked your head. It was almost a hospital trip, but as you'd never been registered . . ."

"We told Wayne to sort it, and he said why not just do what we'd discussed and go. So we did. He gave us cameras and sound gear, and he told us how to set things up. He said to take lots of footage, and to make plans of our house. We were renting, anyway."

"We went to Tasmania, because there are no portals to boo-boo land there," Paul said. "And so, we immersed ourselves in being the Blake family. You howled for bloody Nanny Lu for a few weeks, but we thought you'd forgotten her, the way you forgot Barney."

"It was a good time. We settled in a nice small town and enrolled you into a play group. We'd got well into the swing of it when Wayne showed up and said we'd better get a move on and follow the plan. *What plan?* we said. That's when we found out his idea was a lot more ambitious than what we thought we'd agreed to — which was to create a life and document it for twenty-five years. He said that wouldn't cut it, and if we wouldn't fall into line, he'd have to ask for the money back right away, while there was still time to start with another family. He wanted us to move on every year, to make twenty-five installations, but we finally got him to agree to every two or three. It was awkward. We'd just got you a princess bed and you were not pleased to leave it behind."

"Bloody Nanny Lu all over again," Paul said. "Only this time, it was *bed-bed-bed* till I was sick of the sound of it."

"And so, we went on from there, and shifted to a caravan in Queensland," Adelie said. "We played at being hippies that time. It was fun." She turned to Paul. "Those hairy legs of yours in the daggy dad shorts were an especially choice trademark."

"And you had *Mummy and Co* kids' party entertainment," Paul responded.

"Ah, *Mummy and Co!*" Unexpectedly, Adelie started play-ing air guitar and singing, "*Let the kids glow with Mummy and Co—bake a teddy bear cake out of dinosaur dough . . .*"

"*Play pick-up-sticks with Uncle Max . . .*"

Tamzin glowered at them. "This is no time for *do you re-member.* Why didn't you tell me what was going on?"

Adelie actually put aside her air guitar. "Well . . . you were too young to understand at first, and later it just got easier to let you accept it as the way we lived. We thought it had worked well, aside from a bobble or so like when you went into meltdown about leaving that girl in Adelaide. To be fair, I did *try* to cool the friendship as soon as I saw what was hap-pening."

Paul leaned back and crossed his legs. "You were a proper little madam for most of the time we were in Darwin. By the time we'd become Herrick and Burns, we thought it was safe to come back to New South Wales. Sydney was a big place to get lost in. Lucida would have given up on looking for you, and we stayed away from Fiddle Bay—not that you'd remem-ber it."

"And Wayne got you into a good school where they didn't ask too many questions . . ."

"And blow me, but the damned school took you to Fiddle Bay for an excursion. We really dropped the ball on that one," Adelie mused.

"Easy to do when you're in corporate mode," Paul soothed. He turned back to Tamzin. "After that, you started with the elves again! What the hell triggered that I don't know. And you got mixed up with that boy—Declan. We didn't want an-other situation like the one in Adelaide, so we pulled the plug early."

"But you bolted anyway," Adelie said. She smacked her hands together and made a brushing movement. "Not even a note."

"Did you ever look for me?"

"Well . . . your dad popped back into Guy Herrick mode and went by our old place to see if a delivery had been made there by mistake. Vicki Finchley said no . . . she didn't mention having seen you, and she didn't ask questions."

"She didn't even ask for a forwarding address," Paul said, shaking his head. "That woman had disengagement at a whole new level. And there was I, all prepared with a Herrick-and-Burns email address for her to get in touch if a *delivery* showed up."

"So, you gave up on me."

CHAPTER TWO: BREADCRUMBS

Tamzin Herrick, Adelaide, March 1st, 2020

Adelie said, "*You* were the one who ran out on us. Wayne put out some feelers — even checked back in Adelaide — but he didn't find anything. Where the hell did you go?"

Tamzin ignored that question. She rather enjoyed the idea of Shades looking for her in Adelaide while she was enjoying herself with the clan *over there*.

"You stayed on there, in Macquarie Bay, though. I thought you might move on quickly rather than have to explain why Rochelle never came home to visit."

Adelie said slowly, "I admit we had to be creative. You'd be surprised how much small talk revolves around people's partners and kids, even if the other party barely knows them. The boss at *Flowers and Showers* used to ask after you — even suggested you might come in for a *mum and daughter photo shoot* for a Mother's Day promotion. I had to say you were off on a course . . . and after that I suggested you'd met up with a girlfriend and got a job in Perth. I went off *to spend a week with our daughter* three times after you left. We had emails from *rochelleamarlow* at virtualink dot com, complete with photos, to show off if anyone asked. You rang me twice at work. You might be interested to know you had a virtual cat called Fub — and a website devoted to him."

"I'm glad it was virtual, at least," Tamzin said drily.

Adelie nodded. "After the fuss you made about the peke, I thought I'd better stress that."

"Why keep up the fiction of *Rochelle in Perth*? Why not just move on?"

An odd expression flitted over Adelie's face.

Regret? Sorrow?

"We hoped you'd come back, and we didn't want to be gone when you did," she said.

Tamzin noted that daughter-regret had lasted for possibly two years.

Adelie went on, "That's why we put the bit about *hoping to hear from Rochelle soon* in the exhibition spiel."

"We kept our *DonandMilly* email address, just in case," Paul added.

"Did you never think to email us, just to let us know you were okay?" Adelie asked wistfully.

"No. I didn't even know you had that email address. Why would I? You don't email people you live with."

"*We* do," Paul said.

"God, do you?"

Besides, I was off in fairyland where email isn't a thing.

Paul took up the tale. "We came to Parson Bay for our last couple of years, and we tried something a bit more out there, to ring the changes. We even got a dog."

"I suppose you didn't want to be spotted by anyone who knew you in Sydney or in Fiddle Bay."

"Exactly. You could have knocked us down with a feather when Breezy got invited to a party and who should be there but *you.*"

Ada leaned forward, her Lycra shining again under the coffee shop lighting. "I wasn't sure at first. Most of those dog women called you *Elfie.* They'd talk about their club artist, and some of them showed me paintings you'd done. Then one of them referred to you as *Tamzin.* That's an uncommon name. You looked the right age, and you were musical and painting fantasy stuff, so I risked asking a bloke about you at the party. He said you'd done that whopping big portrait of the hostess and that no, it wasn't him she was sitting on. I got the impression a lot of people thought it might be and he was fed up with explaining. I hoped to have a quick word with you, but you left early.

"By then our time was nearly up. Wayne had got on to us about finalising the gig a couple of years ago. We took a few side trips to look over the stuff we'd put in storage, and to choose the rooms to display, then we came down here to help set up the installations."

"And I must say, it's been a trip," Paul said, absently rubbing his cheek. "I don't think we ever believed it would wind up, did we Penguin?"

"I still can't believe it," Adelie said.

Tamzin thought of Fou, who had served his purpose and whom they had dumped without a qualm. What had Florida termed it? A soft abandonment.

But they didn't abandon me – not quite. They left a few bread-crumbs.

She said, "And now it is wound up, what do you intend to do? Are you going to live as the Lycra-Chaucers for the rest of your lives?"

Paul smiled, and she saw a flash of *Daddy,* who had smelled of pipe tobacco and peppermints, and funny Uncle Mac with his gawky knees and leather sandals. "We haven't made up our minds – Alexandra. The exhibition will run for a good while, because we have so much more material that we can drip feed into the system. There's potential to run other rooms, and to make blank floorplans, and fill them slowly. We have masses of recordings. We can update and make it a *Project Thirty,* or *Project Fifty.*"

"It will be more difficult now the exhibition is open," Adelie said, thoughtfully.

"Because people might be on the lookout for you?" Tamzin asked.

"Great challenge." Paul rubbed his hands together like a pantomime villain. Daddy and Uncle Mac vanished. Now he was Mister Sinister again. "We did the two women thing — we could be two blokes, parent and child — fancy a gymslip, Penguin?"

"*No*," Ada said.

"Okay, that might be a step too far. Wheelchair? You could be my ga-ga granny."

"*No*," Ada repeated. She added, "We might arrange for you to be in callipers."

"Too restrictive. We could always go back to one of our old spots and take up where we left off."

"The Blakes revisited. I liked being them." Ada smiled and tilted her head.

Mummy, the way I first remember her.

Angie pangie, Blaking a pie, Tamzin sang, but only in her head.

"Or come clean and write another book. *Masquerade — the Project Twenty-Five Story*. We could hit the talk show circuit."

"Run workshops on reinvention."

They beamed in unison, and Tamzin saw they had no regrets for the way they'd lived. They were still full of ideas and plans. They were still delighted with themselves and with one another.

She was suddenly rather tired.

She turned to Adelie. "I always used to think you were straightforward. You gave me rules and consequences, and what you said you'd do, you did. That was stability of a kind — right up until the day of my formal, when you broke your promise to take me shopping for a dress."

"Water under the bridge," Paul said airily.

Tamzin said, "Do you *want* to wear that cake?"

"I've told you that's an irritating comment," Adelie said.

Tamzin continued, "If I ask you to give me your word about something in writing now, will you do it?"

Adelie nodded. "I will. If I give my word today, I'll keep it. If I can't promise that, I won't give it." She looked expectantly at Tamzin. "You've turned out *so* well, Alexandra."

"I think so, too," Tamzin said. She added, without premeditation, "Why all the poets' names? Why the A-names and the one-syllable names?"

"Continuity," Adelie said.

"In-joke," Paul said at the same time. "We'll be waiting to see who first spots it in the exhibition."

Tamzin said, "Ada."

"Ada? I never had that one."

"Okay, Mum, then. Adelie. Penguin. I want your word that you won't adopt any more pets and treat them the way you did Fou. You even deprived him of his bear!"

"Which unaccountably disappeared, only to reappear, somehow newer," Paul said, looking hard at Matin. "I detect *your* fine elfin hand in that. I suspect Wayne underestimated *you*, big time, Matty-the-elf-boy."

Tamzin said, "Shut up, Mister Sinister."

"*Mister Sinister?*"

"Shut up, whoever you are." She returned her gaze to Adelie. "Also, you will agree that Fou is my dog in perpetuity and that you have no claim on him." She glanced at Matin. "Can you get me a notebook?"

Matin clicked his fingers and handed her a pad and pencil.

Tamzin nodded her thanks and scribbled down a sentence. She pushed the pad across to her mother, who read it, and initialled it, using her original name.

She looked expectantly at Tamzin, as if waiting for thanks, or for the next request. Instead, Tamzin returned the pad and pencil to Matin, who dismissed them.

"That's all?" Adelie said, sounding surprised.

"Yes." Tamzin drained her tea. "That cake looks good, Matin. Can you send our share back to the *Harvest Hob*—but not where Fou or Riannan can get it? It has chocolate in it."

He raised his hand, and two of the pieces of cake vanished.

Tamzin smiled at him, pushed back her chair and got to her feet. She held out her hand to Matin. "Let's go and see how the Twenty-Twenty-Vision exhibition is going."

Matin got up and put his arm around her.

"That's it?"

Did Adelie sound dismayed? Tamzin said, "There's nothing else to say, is there?"

"Nothing about keeping out of your way and not meddling in your lives?" Mister Sinister asked. She'd decided that was a better name for him than Paul.

Tamzin shrugged. "No. That would imply that I care enough to bother avoiding you."

"Ouch," Adelie said softly.

"If you want to keep in touch with me, you can always contact me via my *Elf-Made Art* website or through Branok St Ives, my solicitor who, if you care to know, offered, along with his wife, to adopt me in case I ever needed visible parents." She paused to let that sink in. "If you're using another name, ask me if I ever paint peace lilies, so I'll know it's you. *If*, and I mean if, you ever want a relationship with your grandchildren, you will need to revert to your Herrick and Burns identity for the term of any visit or visual contact. You won't be having our children for sleepovers because I could never trust you not to flit. I can't and won't spend any more time chasing you. The ball is in your court."

Matin handed her two business cards — one for *Elf-Made Art* and the other for *Arts in Tune.* She flipped them onto the table.

"Goodbye Mum, Dad. I might see you around."

Matin nodded to them. "Mister Bysshe-Minister. Miss Spenser. It was good to meet you."

"Oh, was it indeed?" Mister Sinister said. He pointed at Matin. "Don't think we didn't notice you sitting there all superior and disapproving, Matty-the-elf-boy."

"I do disapprove of the way you treated your daughter," Matin said.

"You people can't take the moral high ground . . . you come here and pretend to be human. You get jobs and drive cars — what for? Why can't you just stay in boo-boo land and skip through the daisies?"

"You should ask Master Ellington that," Matin said calmly. "But I'd leave it a while. He might not be in the best position to answer you right now."

They turned and left the coffee shop.

"All right, my dolphin?" Matin asked as they stepped into the balmy open air.

"Yes, oddly enough. I haven't even got the inner trembles."

They walked on.

As they headed for Gallery Paterson, Tamzin said, "Matin, you said you'd tell me what you did to Wayne Ellington."

"I know, but if I tell you, your opinion of me might suffer a downturn."

"Tell me anyway. You had my back in there, and I'll never forget you promised to use a compulsion if they wouldn't talk."

"I didn't need to." He sounded mildly disappointed. "They seemed willing to explain."

"They were positively loquacious. I don't think it would have been as easy if I'd tracked them down before. Do you remember, I once implied I blamed you because I came home too late to be with Dequan?"

He assented.

"Eventually, I realised it was nothing to do with anything you did. It was my wish — I wished to stay *over there* until it was time to be Tamzin again. And now I have my time. And Ada and Mister Sinister have completed their twenty-five years of living created lives as an art installation and are presumably well out of range of whatever their initial problem was. It's done, so they considered themselves free to talk to me. It was the perfect time to find them, after the exhibition opening but before they had time to vanish again." She smiled with satisfaction. "It was time to solve the mystery. And now, it's time for me to find out what you did to Shades."

Matin said, "Have you ever heard of a willy-tingler?"

Tamzin felt her eyes widen.

"I see you have."

"Shay mentioned it to me once."

"It would have to be your Shay," he said with a grin.

"Mind, it was only to say he didn't need one."

"I'm sure he doesn't. How many children do he and Honoreé have, now?"

"Five—unless they've managed a new one since last July. He did say they wanted another little colleen. But don't change the subject. You mean you put a willy-tingler on Shades?" She stared up at him.

Matin looked sheepish. "I did."

"But that's—that's—"

"Reprehensible," he said.

"No! It's perfect! Oh, I wish I'd seen it! Did he double up and grab at himself?"

Matin said gently, "It wiped the snide look off his face."

"Can he take it off?"

"I doubt it."

"Is there a Mistress Ellington?"

He shrugged. "I hope not, for her sake."

"Well, maybe you should take it off him now."

Matin jerked his free hand back as if hauling on a rope. "Gone. But if he ever calls me *Matty the elf boy* again, or so much as *thinks* of contacting Aunt Mim—"

"You can put it back on." Tamzin looked up at her betrothed in awe. "Daylight was wrong about elf boys. You do *not* lack a spice of evil."

CHAPTER THREE: OUTCOMES AND A PUPPY

Tamzin Herrick, Late May, 2020

Florida Klim and her dog, Harley, met up with Tamzin and Fou at the Dames with Dogs clubhouse by arrangement.

Tamzin smiled a greeting, and Fou made a lazy flip with his tail.

Florida sat down on one of the long padded couches that lined the walls. "So, Elfie, have you resigned yourself to being owned by a peke?"

Tamzin patted the peke in question, carefully avoiding his toy bear, which had acquired a whole new level of slobber and grime. "I have."

"Did you ever find out where Breezy and Clem ended up after their flit?"

Tamzin said, "Would it surprise you enormously to be told that Breezy and Clem never really existed?"

Florida removed her padded helmet and laid it carefully beside her on the bench. "I never saw that coming. I mean, I know Breezy, although I couldn't say we were ever friends. Care to explain, Elfie?"

"I would. It will sound unbelievable to you, but I guarantee it's the truth as far as I know it."

"You might be surprised at what a Dame with Dogs can believe," Florida said. She glanced betrayingly at Caddy Hildebrand and Pud Greenhow. Caddy's mother was human, but her father was a venerable elf man from Windhill. Pud's lineage was pure hob. Neither of them had ever mentioned their heritage to Tamzin, but Daylight had enlightened her about Pud. She'd already guessed about Caddy.

"I doubt if any Dame could surprise me now," Tamzin said. "The fact is, Breezy was a construct. She isn't European, or Canadian or whatever else people think. She's an Australian-born woman. Her birth name was Adelie Jane Spenser. I don't know what the status of that name is now. She hasn't used it since the mid nineteen-nineties. As for Clem, *she's* not American or Canadian either. She's not even a *she*. No, not trans, or anything like that. Just another construct, because their original identities lived at Fiddle Bay, so making them both women added an extra layer of obfuscation.

"Clem's original name was Paul Bysshe-Minister. Same deal as with Breezy. I don't know the legal status of a name that's been abandoned but never officially changed, do you?"

Florida shook her head. "Where are they now?"

"I have no idea. They might be calling themselves Ayesha and Joe Chaucer, and dressing in Lycra and riding carbon fibre bikes, or maybe not. About the only thing you can say for certain is that *her* name will begin with A, even if she's using a nickname that doesn't, the one *he* uses will have one syllable, even if it's officially longer, and their surname will belong to a British poet — or two poets, if they're not being Mister and Missus. In any case, they said I can keep Fou."

Florida pursed her lips in a soundless whistle. Tamzin quite saw it was a lot to take in.

"Where did you find them — and how?"

"At a gallery in Adelaide. I'd love to say it was grand detective work, but I have a suspicion they *let* me find them. It's too complicated to sort out and I'm not going to try. I cornered them with cream cake and obliged them to explain themselves. They owed me."

"I should think so, leaving you holding the peke."

"Not only that. They owed me because they're my parents. At least—I believe so, and they didn't deny it. They had the audacity to say I'd turned out well!"

Florida choked. "What did you say?"

Tamzin grinned at her. "I agreed. And no, I didn't know I was looking for my parents when I went seeking two gay ladies in capes who had left me with a temporary lodger and no contact details. I found out through channels which, just like the pathway to meeting, are too long and tortuous to sail down today. But now you know. For the record, I was born on New Year's Day nineteen ninety-three, and my birth name was Alexandra Spenser. Believe me?"

"It's too bizarre not to believe."

"That's what I think. Are you ready to go?"

Florida got up again. "Sure. Does Daylight know all this?"

"No. You and Matin, my purported parents, their facilitator, and my solicitor and his wife are the only ones who know at present. I'll tell Daylight sometime."

With the dogs in the back of her van and Florida beside her, Tamzin drove out of Windhill and back through the city to the house Daylight now shared with Garret Rosebay.

Daylight was waiting for them. "I don't know what to do about Banbury Cross," she said, by way of greeting.

"Why? Is it peeling?" Tamzin glanced at the huge canvas. It looked fine to her.

Daylight laid a hand on her flat stomach. "It's perfect, but I'm not sure it will be appropriate to have it on the wall when Daffodil arrives."

"Didn't you say you'd never call a child Daffodil?"

Daylight smiled brilliantly. "Tamzdie, darling, my husband really does want to call her Daffodil. What can I say?"

"That's your problem. You might consider *yes*, considering the dance you led him. Congratulations on your joint achievement, anyway."

"Thank you. I think we planted her on our first wedding night. I was certainly yelling *yes* rather a lot, so maybe Gar took that as permission to plant a daffodil."

"I think it's a charming name," Florida said.

"Do you really?"

"I do. I have a flower name myself, after all."

Daylight and Tamzin both stared at her.

"Flora," Florida said cheerfully. "Thought you knew."

"Oh." Daylight glanced at the small painting Tamzin had done for her as a wedding present for her official wedding two months before, and she changed the subject. "Have you and Cam set the date yet?"

"No. Do you think you could call him *Matin?* It is his name."

"No point promising what I can't deliver. I've known him since he was a fluffy little apprentice at *Wildwood*, hanging with Otto and Gar and getting under Terry's feet. He's always been Cam to me."

Tamzin gave up on that one. "Would you like me to paint some clothes onto Banbury Cross to spare your blushes?"

"That would be a pity. No, I think maybe we'll move it to our new sitting room and put curtains in front of it with a glamour that can be lifted when we have someone we want to impress."

"Good plan."

Florida didn't react to Daylight's comment about a glamour, but she said, "We didn't come to talk about paintings, or to name your baby. We came to pick a pup for my sister. I said she ought to do it herself, but she asked me to—she's such a softie she's probably afraid she'd fall in love with the whole litter and end up with six of them."

"Five. We're keeping one. They're in the back room. Go on through while I get tea—you can take Harley and Fou. Shelley won't mind a bit. Our pup is the boy with the two black paws. We're calling him Cherry Pie von Atapeke. The others are up for grabs — to suitable homes, naturally."

"I can vouch for my sister's home being suitable," Florida said.

Tamzin and Florida headed to the back room, where Shelley's litter of six pups rolled and toddled about, growling shrilly.

Fou sniffed noses with Shelley, while Harley poked his nose into the tumble of warm little bodies.

"This one," Florida said, pouncing on a fat pup with one white paw.

Daylight came in with a tray of tea. "Good choice. He's a laid-back little guy," she approved. She added, "Not like Atapeke, who is going to be hell on wheels."

"Why are you keeping him, then? Surely Daffodil will be enough of a handful?"

"We're keeping him because Shelley insists. She says she wouldn't know a moment's peace if she didn't know exactly what Atapeke was up to at all times. She says she simply cannot have him out in the world trashing her reputation."

Since Shelley was a perfectly normal dog, aside from being placid for a Jack Russell, Tamzin took that proclamation with a very large grain of salt.

Fou sniffed his offspring one at a time. He returned twice to a little bitch with a brindled ear. Her stubby tail already gave promise of a fine Pekingese arch.

"Another good choice by the man in the frame." Daylight bent, picked up the pup and bundled her into Tamzin's arms. "This is a wedding present," she said.

"Thank you," Tamzin said. "I'm going to call her Shoe."

"What kind of name is that?" Daylight asked.

"It's a mash-up of Shelley and Fou." It was also a tribute to her spy-heeled shoes that had carried her through so many adventures, but she felt no need to mention that. "By the way, who said I wanted a puppy? We came to get one for Florida's sister."

"Tamzdie, you know you want one . . . Fou's your lodger. You absolutely need a dedicated dog, so you won't be bereft when he goes home."

"Fou *is* my dedicated dog, and he *is* home. I have it in writing."

Daylight puffed out her cheeks. "I'm glad. So now you have two dedicated dogs, daddy and daughter." She added, "Three down, three to go. That means I can tell the other three Dames who put their hands up for a Jackapeke to come tomorrow and pick theirs. Or maybe I'll sit the Dames down and let the pups pick." She dusted off her hands and grinned at them. "And that, my friends, is how to sort your dogs."

Tamzin noted that marriage with Garret Rosebay and a baby-in-waiting hadn't changed her mad friend a bit. She was glad about that.

After taking Florida to deliver the pup to her sister, Tamzin had three hours on hand before she met up with Matin. They were going to dinner with Matin's family at Bellflower Cottage. She had arranged to take possession of Shoe the next day, so she parked near a station, and caught a train. She intended to visit Gillan St Ives, who was deep in preparation for her sons' weddings and who wanted to discuss portraits for her expanding family, but instead, she got off at Circular Quay.

Fou, in his usual phlegmatic fashion, pottered along by her side, occasionally glancing up to make sure Tamzin had his disreputable toy bear in her shoulder-bag. Since he'd been reunited with it in March, he insisted on it being in scenting range at all times.

Tamzin reflected that once Shoe joined their family, life might become a bit more complicated, but now she was free of the mystery that had clouded her life for so long, she had flung open the doors of opportunity. She knew, without pondering the matter, that Shoe was a good idea. Fou was well into middle age, and she was somewhat haunted by what her friend Nell's husband had said about their elderly chihuahua.

I don't know what we'll do when Pepe's gone where good dogs go . . .

She walked on autopilot, thinking of all the possibilities for the next couple of hours. She could catch a ferry over to Gilchrist and have coffee at *Paws a While* with Rev and Pud. She could settle in a park and begin some sketches for the story Emily had sent her . . . a story of a girl who walked into a world of fantasy. Did Emily *know*? Tamzin had kept her promise to reveal the secret of her disappearance back when she was Jade Eliot. She had kept it brief, recommending that Emily should visit Gallery Spenser for further enlightenment.

A flash of purple caught her eye and she glanced at a rack of coloured scarves forming a rainbow arch over a shop doorway.

Fairings.

CHAPTER FOUR: FAIRINGS

Tamzin Herrick, Late May, 2020

Tamzin's feet stuttered to a stop.

Fairings – the small boutique where she had made a hasty purchase of a dress for her formal, all those years ago, was real and it was here.

She stood there, with Fou by her side, tossing up on whether to go in. Should she risk another disappointment such as she'd had when she visited *Oranges and Lemons*?

Nice Mister Orange and Miss Lemon were long gone, and the new owner was oddly disengaged.

But I did get three of Emily's books, and now we're working together again. How bad could it be?

She picked up Fou. If the owner barred dogs, which would be perfectly reasonable, she'd take it as a sign.

Holding the peke to her bosom, she stepped into the shop, accompanied by a chime of silver bells that sent a shiver down her spine.

I know that tune . . . it's Matin's lullaby.

She looked about at the racks of dresses and shawls, scarves and flowing pants.

The woman behind the counter looked up from where she was stitching applique on a blouse. She was probably in her fifties, wearing a flowing dress in a bewildering range of purples from the palest lavender to the rich hue of violets. Her brown hair was caught up in a loose bun, and she had hazel eyes. She smelled of some elusive floral perfume. *Le bouquet des fees.*

"Hello," she said, setting her needle safely into a fold of the cloth and laying her work aside.

Tamzin said, "Greet you, mistress. I'm sure you don't remember me, but I—"

"I believe your name is Tamzin Herrick," the woman said. "Don't look so startled. It's not magic, and my memory is no better than average."

"Enlighten me." She supposed she sounded short, but she was done with mysteries.

The woman said, "I went to South Australia for Mother's Day this year, and while I was there, my daughter took me to see the Twenty-Twenty Vision exhibition. She told me two of the exhibitors were from hereabouts, and at least five of them were fay-touched. You come into both those categories. I recognise you from your self-portrait."

"I hope you enjoyed the exhibition."

"I did. The floral platter gave me an idea for a *queen of the flowers* fabric that features meadow flowers rather than roses. I had a good reason to be interested in your picture, though. The dress you wore in the major image came from here. I always recognise my own work. I can see the charms."

Tamzin said, "I bought it years ago when I was seventeen. I came in just before closing time and you sold it to me at a discount because it was the only green dress you had."

"I remember." The woman held up her hand. "Again, *not* because of magic, but because my son mentioned to me that he'd seen a girl wearing one of my creations. At the behest of one of his young workmates, he facilitated a wish for her. For you, I mean. It seemed to trouble him."

Tamzin paused to work this out. The woman was certainly not Matin's mother, Lirrin, who was slim and ethereal looking, and whom she knew well and loved already. That meant she had to be—"Are you Mistress Fairling?" she asked.

"I don't often get accorded that honorific *over here.* My

name's Jacaranda Fairling, yes. You are the young woman who encountered my son, Orlando, a decade ago. He didn't tell me anything about you in detail, I might add — not even your name — just that you were wearing a dress from my shop when he last saw you. Do you still have it?"

"Yes! I wear it a lot. My betrothed likes it."

"He has good taste. It still fits well?"

"Matin told me it would always fit, because it's charmed."

"Up to a point. If you put on a great deal of weight, it wouldn't, but you look to me like someone who won't do that."

Tamzin considered Ada and Mister Sinister, who must be into their fifties, but who were not abashed to wear form-fitting Lycra. If nothing else, they had given her good physical genes as well as adaptability.

"How may I help you today?" Jacaranda Fairling asked.

"I saw the shop as I was passing, and I wondered if it was still the way I remembered. I went into a bookshop I used to love in Adelaide. It was under new management, and it had changed a lot."

"And has *Fairings* changed from your perspective?"

"Yes, I think so, but the ambience is still the same, because you're still here."

"I have no plans to sell," Jacaranda said.

"I'm glad. While I'm here, do you have wedding gowns? I don't want anything too elaborate, but I don't want to stand up in my green dress, much as I love it, or in my court ballgown. I want to shine in something new."

"I'm sure we can arrange that. What order is your man?"

"He's an elf, but I'm human."

"Are you marrying in the formal human style?"

Tamzin recalled the conversation she'd had with Branok St Ives before she found out her original name. Even now, she was unsure of her legal status. Mister Sinister and Ada had implied that her birth had never been registered and she was certainly not marrying in the name she had been given initially. Alexandra Spenser was a lovely name, but it wasn't *her*.

"We thought a fay priest might be best."

"Then I could probably make something up for you. I doubt if any of the gowns I have here would be quite right. Have you anything in mind?"

Tamzin said, "I'll be wearing my pendant and my bracelet, and these shoes."

"If you lower your dog, I might be able to see the pendant," Jacaranda Fairling said. She sounded a wee bit amused.

"Is it okay if I put him down? He'll behave."

"I'll call my assistant to take him out to the workroom for a drink. Don't worry. She has a fine touch with dogs and children." She put her head through some drapes at the back of the shop. "Luce? Would you like to take care of a little dog for a few minutes?" She glanced back at Tamzin. "What's his name?"

"Fou."

The woman who came through from the workroom looked like a startled hare. She looked briefly at Tamzin before she held out her hands to Fou.

"Come here to Luce, my lovely." She had a musical voice, and Tamzin wondered if she sang.

Jacaranda nodded encouragingly to Tamzin. "He'll be fine with Luce."

Tamzin said, "She'll need to take this bear as well." She extracted the toy from her bag.

"Just a few minutes, Luce. Then he needs to come back to Tamzin," Jacaranda said, and the woman nodded and carried Fou away.

"All right, let me size you up." Jacaranda looked Tamzin over. "If you're wearing that wooden pendant, you won't want tulle and silk. In fact, a light colour would swallow the bracelet." She focused on the shoes and gestured for Tamzin to sit. "May I?"

Tamzin sat and removed her shoes. Jacaranda, kneeling without the least difficulty, picked them up and examined them.

She laughed in apparent delight. "I can see why you want to wear these! They're leprechaun work, and very artful."

Tamzin nodded. "They used to belong to my betrothed's sister. Her godfather made them, but she gave them to me . . . though not directly." She added, "What did you mean when you said they were artful?"

"They're charmed for luck, but you obviously know that already. They're also charmed for secrets. Those heels are hollow."

Tamzin said wryly, "They've guarded a few secrets for me in my time. Only in one heel, though."

"Oh?"

"I've only ever been able to open one. Although — goodness, I just remembered Matin, my betrothed, did say the other one should open too."

"I expect it will when the time comes. Now, I can see a couple of possibilities here. You could choose one of the colours in these beauties. You'd look lovely in violet. You might want to avoid green, since you already have a green dress from me. Red might not be what you want for a wedding."

"What's the other option?" Tamzin asked.

"You could use all the colours, layered the way they are on the shoes. If you had a low, square neckline, the pendant would clear it. It would need to be a simple design."

Tamzin thought of the beautiful dress Pen Inkersoll had worn to the Twenty-Twenty Vision opening. She took a notepad and pencil out of her bag, and sketched Pen's dress with its flowing lines, changed her mind and substituted a plain, long-sleeved tunic. "Something like this? I think the fijordfee flicken wear this style, so you probably know it."

The woman nodded. "I do, although we don't see many of them *over here*. Possibly a base in a solid colour, with a layer of shifting colours over it."

"That sounds lovely." It sounded bizarre, but she had no doubt Otto's mother would make something beautiful. Her own dress, with its harmonising shades, was a testament to her skill. Daringly, she asked, "Are you making dresses for your son's brides?"

Jacaranda's eyes crinkled in a smile. "I am. They both chose the same colour, a light hydrangea blue, but I'm adding embroidery to differentiate them — Flanders poppy for Kim and sprigs of rosemary for Charlotte. When are you getting married?"

"Soon," Tamzin said. She was a few months younger than she'd estimated, but she was ready to move on and up.

"I could have your dress made by mid-June if that would be soon enough."

Two weeks?

"That sounds perfect. How much will it be? I do know a custom-made dress will be more expensive than something off the peg."

"I would normally charge in the human scale, since I pay rates and taxes like anyone else, but in your case, I would do the job for a peppercorn sum on condition you allow me to use your picture to display. Your dress will be, and will remain, one of a kind, but I like to show inspirational pictures to clients."

"That's too generous of you. I'm sure you get as much work as you can handle already."

"It will be a pleasure to dress you, my dear. My son has always fretted that he could have done better for you in the matter of the wish."

"What he did was exactly what I needed, even if I didn't understand that at the time," Tamzin said. She added, "He threw me in to sink or swim, but I needed that. I'd been frozen and hopeless for months. I woke up in the place he left me, and I saw two beautiful men. Their kindness, and their families' acceptance of a temporary member, gave me the courage to move on when I needed to. Your son also gave me courage. He told me I would be safe from deliberate harm. That gave me the freedom to grasp what life offered me."

"Have you told him that?"

"Not in so many words. We've never actually acknowledged our previous acquaintance. I used to see him now and again, but my betrothed doesn't work with him now."

"Then may I tell him?"

"Certainly. I owe so much to so many people, and I should have thanked more of them along the way."

"Not to worry. He couldn't be happier now he's finally sorted out what — who — he wants. He was pining for a — how did you put it — a *temporary* young woman for a while, but now he's found forevers. I didn't expect him to end up with *two,* but I suppose he couldn't choose between them. They're both dear maids, great friends who play off one another. Otto's a fortunate man."

Tamzin laughed. "Two can be wonderful, but he might need a bit more stamina than most."

Jacaranda, understandably, reverted hastily to the matter of Tamzin's dress. "I could photograph you when you come for your fitting, or —" She broke off, looking hopefully at Tamzin.

"Or I could paint a self-portrait in the dress."

Jacaranda nodded serenely. "A mirrored portrait would be perfect. Is it a deal?"

I should talk this over with Matin or ask Gillan's advice. Or even run it past Daylight — she looked so beautiful when she married Garret —

The thought of her mother flashed in and out of her mind. It was weeks since the encounter in *Galleria Coffee.* She had heard and seen nothing of her elusive parents since that day. They had her contact details, but she did not have theirs . . . unless that *DonandMilly* email address still worked.

"It's a deal," she said.

"I'm glad. I love my work, but it's a while since I've felt excited about creating something outstanding. My daughters-to-be are fine maids, but there being two of them is quite unusual enough without dressing them in something too eye-catching. Besides, I'm mother enough to want my son to shine. He's going to be in dark blue with festival embroidery."

Tamzin thought Otto would shine in that all right, and she said so as she resumed her sandals. Having found *Fairings* again, and not wanting to lose it, she put the address into her phone, also writing it in her notebook for good measure. "I'd better go. I'm meeting Matin soon. Fou?"

"I'll call Lucida. She's probably out there singing lullabies to your Fou."

Jacaranda touched a bellpull, and silvery chimes rang out.

The other woman came out, holding Fou and his bear. She paid little attention to Tamzin, but she hugged the peke and said, "Lu loves you, darling Fou. I hope I'll see you again very soon."

"Count on it," Jacaranda said. She turned to Tamzin. "In fact, you might need to keep a good hold on him until you're well away. Our Luce is a bit of a pied piper when it comes to the little ones, right, Luce? They always want to stay with you and bathe in your love."

The woman smiled obliquely. She handed Fou over to Tamzin and ducked back through the curtain.

Jacaranda said, "Lucida has a lovely touch with small beings. Some people find her odd, but she cared for my youngest daughter after school for years. They had a habit of going off on what Fidelia termed *green adventures,* but they always came home eventually. Luce's mind might be a little northwest of normal, but I trust her implicitly."

CHAPTER FIVE: COME TO ME

Tamzin Herrick, Late May, 2020

Tamzin and Fou caught the train back to the club house, and Tamzin drove to the castle bridge gate, where Matin was waiting to take her through to Bellflower Cottage to spend the evening with the rest of his family.

"Busy day, mistress?" he asked as, hand in hand, they stepped through the gateway and set off for Starside, where the cottage was.

"Interesting," she said. "I have some things to tell you."

"Should I be worried?"

"Not a bit. They're nice things."

The landscape had been blurring around her, but it abruptly swam into focus.

Here already?

They weren't. Tamzin looked about her. "Where are we?"

"Don't you know?"

"It looks a bit familiar . . ." Away to her left were white cottages with neat gardens, and meadows divided by drystone walls. Two donkeys saw her and brayed a welcome.

"Do you know now?" Matin asked.

"Yes, it's Balla Cloiche village." She looked at him in surprise. "Matin, you *do* know a good many of the gossoons here proposed marriage to me?"

"I believe you said so."

"Mind you, they'll have forgotten me by now."

"Niver a bit of it, darlin' Thomasine," a voice said

cheerfully from behind her.

Tamzin turned to look over her shoulder. It was close to three years since she'd used that name, and much more than that since she'd spent time at this village waiting to board the galleon with Nuala Lightheart.

Leprechaun men, with their green skin, hair that ranged from sandy-fair to red, and their habit of wearing green or brown britches and tunics, tended to look alike to the untrained eye, but Tamzin had painted a great many of the Balla Cloiche gossoons.

This one, though — she looked at him hard as he unfolded from where he'd been sitting in the shade of one of the walls. "You'll be one of Nuala's brothers," she said.

"Sure, I'm Tiernan Flute," he said. "I niver proposed marriage or anything else to ye, but ye were kind enough to compliment me playing back when I was so high." He held a hand at shoulder height. "But where's your fiddle? Have ye traded it for that *madra beag*?" He indicated Fou.

"No, I have it at home. I'd have brought it along if I'd known I was coming here," Tamzin said, shooting a glance at Matin.

"Your man did not see fit to tell ye? Sure, 'twas an arrangement we made." He clicked his fingers to Fou and crouched to give the dog a rub on the head. If the peke found a small young man with green skin anything to blink at, he failed to betray it.

"My man did not." She switched her attention back to her betrothed. "Matin, why are we here? Do you *know* Master Flute?"

The young man gave her an impish look as he bounced to his feet. "If ye've a mind to scold him, I can give ye a while to twist some sense into his bollocks."

"I'm not scolding him. And by the way, I use Tamzin for my name now."

"So your man said, but to me ye're bright-eyed Thomasine, who lifted me young heart right out of me breast and kissed it."

"Oh, get along with you," Tamzin said, knowing blarney when she heard it. "I'm sure you have plenty of colleens waiting to throw you a come-to-me—or maybe one has already."

"So I should, if they were not blood of my blood in this village and the next. I was off wid the ships to cast for a colleen at Erin a'Fee, but Nuala sent me word of a sweet darlin' sailing my way on her say-so." He kissed his fingers. "Three weeks more and she'll be here, and if we like what we see . . . we'll kiss in friendship and more." He grinned at her. "Then, it's off we'll be in clover."

"I hope things go well for you," she said.

"They will, if she's as fine a colleen as Nuala tells it." He folded his arms, still grinning.

Tamzin thought it would be a cold-hearted colleen who would resist this young man if he turned on the blarney. Besides, she must be at least three-quarters committed to the match to be already on her way.

"But I'm not here to talk o' my affairs, darlin'," he said.

"No?"

"Not a bit of it. I'm here on your man's business." He nodded to Matin. "He was by here asking for news o' Nuala Lightheart, and who better to give it than a brother o' her blood and her heart? She was here for a visit back in summer—had a good man to hold her an' two babbies as proof of his attentions. Swellin' with another, too! One she calls Rose an' the other is Thomasine, so ye see she's niver forgotten ye."

"I'm so glad she found what she wanted," Tamzin said. She had liked Nuala, with her clear-eyed pragmatism about arranging her life.

"There, then! If ye'd wish to see her again, come here in summer when she'll be back to show off her new babby to

Mammy and Da," he said. He put his fingers into the pocket of his britches and took out a shamrock pin. "This is a come-to-me, from her to me to you. It will bring ye back here, come the time."

Tamzin took the pin, puzzling over the complexities of the fay favour system. Nuala wanted to see her again, but her brother had acted as proxy, and so —

"What may I offer for a thank-you?"

Tiernan said easily, "It pleases me to help me sister, and sure, ye did pay me a compliment years ago. If ye feel the need though, a kiss will pay me well — if your man can be kept from kicking me backside into next week and me bollocks along wid it."

"Matin's an elf, not a pixie, so your backside and your bollocks are safe," Tamzin said. She gave the gossoon a hug and a kiss, having to bend a little to do it. He smelled of clover and new bread, and she thought his colleen, when she came, would be happy to love him. "Road rise, Tiernan Flute, and may you have arms around you soon," she said.

That was a blessing her onetime lover Shay had given her, and now she passed it on.

Tiernan, his duty done, headed back to the village, and Matin took Tamzin's hand.

"You did wonder what became of your friend," he said.

"And now I know. It will be good to meet her again and I thank you for arranging this. You know, I've been thinking of her, when I do think of her, living far away over the ocean. Why didn't it ever occur to me that of *course* she comes back to see her people here? Leprechauns like to keep tabs on their families, and since they don't conjure, they must visit more than most. But how did you know where to come?"

Matin said, "I asked my godfather, Eamon the Red, but he has never been to Balla Cloiche. Nor has Lugh Traveller, who is his da, you know. Therefore, I went to Dancing Tor and found your Shay. He didn't know, but he said be sure his da would, and sure enough Master Treelove has a cousin's cousin-by-love living in the next village along. And by the way, Master Treelove wishes you a joyful heart and hopes you might come to play the fiddle with him one day, so he can be sure it is still in tune."

"What did you tell him?"

"I said it was up to you, but with Winterwatch coming up in a few weeks, you might easily take a side trip to visit your clan."

"I might."

"What's the worst that can happen?" he asked.

"Juliette might be still displeased with me, as well as with Kate."

"Let her be . . . but if I come with you, then she'll see her precious son is in no danger from your charms. It is time she put that hurt behind her, for her sake as well as for yours."

"I don't know why she was so upset with me. I *did* leave him to Briar, so they could marry and have babies. Grand-babies were what she wanted."

"That's probably the key to it. *You* left *him*. If he'd tired of you there would be no issue in her mind."

"I didn't *tire* of him. I never *tired* of any of my boys. It was just time for me to move on and for them to find their forevers who would never move on."

"And now you've found your own forever and you'll never move on."

"So long as we both shall live. We may move on, but it will be together. Exactly. Are we going to Skyside now?" she asked as they set off again.

"Yes. The family won't be there, yet, but the godbrothers are waiting to take Fou for a stroll through the meadow. They undertake to remove any resulting burrs from his coat by hand."

"Oh, really."

"I'm sure he needs exercise."

"He's getting it already."

"*I* need exercise," he clarified.

By the time they reached Bellflower Cottage and Matin had delivered Fou into the care of his godfather's sons Ronan and Faolin, Tamzin had almost forgotten the news she had for Matin.

In any case, she had no time to tell him, for he whisked her into the cottage and along to his bedroom where he undressed them both with a click of his fingers, picked her up, and tossed her onto his bed.

Tamzin had barely stopped bouncing on the springyweed mattress before he rolled on top of her and pressed on in. He took her hard and fast, and Tamzin, surprised but pleased, gave herself into his passion, wriggling energetically as if trying to escape.

"What was that about?" she asked, panting, when he rolled off.

Matin's chest was heaving, and he took a few seconds to answer.

"I'm *not* a pixie," he said.

"I know. You're my delicious elf man who smells of green peas. I want to rub mint into your balls and lick you all over. Why would I think you were a pixie?"

"That cheeky gossoon—asking for a kiss."

"Yes, and I gave him a good one. He was a sweet little boy when I knew him before, and he's a sweet young man now. His colleen will be a lucky—" She yelped as Matin pulled her to him again. "Ooh!" she added, purring with pleasure. "Now I know how to get you hot and bothered. All I need is a gossoon to kiss with appropriate enthusiasm. I wonder if the godbrothers would be up for it—"

"Do not—say—*up* for it!" Matin groaned and shuddered as

he spilled. He went on shaking and Tamzin pushed back to peer into his face.

Surely, he knows I'm joking.

To her relief, he was laughing. He gave her a swat on the bottom, and she blew a raspberry into his neck.

"Round three?" she suggested, twiddling his cock.

He said, "Later. Speaking of the godbrothers, they'll be back with Fou soon, and I think I heard Olivier and Nessa come in halfway through round two."

"Better get decent then," Tamzin said. She looked about for her dress, but when Matin obligingly re-dressed her, she was wearing an old fay tunic she kept at the cottage.

"Knickers?" she asked, having ascertained he hadn't provided those.

Matin shook his head. "I might want you again halfway through dinner and need a quick trip to the meadow."

"And I might want *you* for dessert. Can we spend the night here?"

"I'm counting on it," he said.

Tamzin tidied her hair and walked demurely out to the sitting room, where Olivier and his pisky love, Nessa Tremayne, were kissing on the sofa.

Olivier lifted his head to say, "Greet you, sister-by-love. Your dog's here somewhere."

"Down in the cellar with the godbrothers," Nessa said. Her eyes were dilated and her hair so messy Tamzin wondered why she had bothered to tidy her own.

"What are they doing down there?" she asked.

"Playing with their poteen, I think. They made a new batch—even more horrible than the last."

A squeal of glee from the door heralded the arrival of Dickon Haydale, whose command of his feet far outweighed his command of language.

Tamzin scooped him up for a hug, and kissed Misty, her husband, Lars, Nessa, and a rather startled Olivier.

"What about me?" Matin had emerged from the bedroom.

"I think she already kissed you," Nessa said seriously.

"Did someone speak o' kissin'?" Two green-skinned young men popped up through the cellar trapdoor like pantomime demons. One of them had his arms around Fou, and the other had the stuffed bear dangling from his belt like a trophy.

Tamzin kissed her fingers to them and took possession of the peke and the bear.

"You're very excitable today! Indeed, you're behaving like a hoyden," Misty said, settling into a chair in a welter of layered cambric. She was expecting another baby, but as she always wore voluminous gowns at Bellflower Cottage, it took a knowing eye to tell.

"Says the woman who sits on her man among the turnips during the Hot," Tamzin retorted.

Lars moaned and gave his wife a reproachful look. "Eh, lass!"

Matin said, "She does *what?*"

"A bit bumpy," Nessa observed.

"Tatties are better," the godbrothers chorused.

"Greet you all, my dears," Matin's mother said serenely, as her husband conjured a huge hamper into being on the table near the couch.

Dickon ran to her. "Ganny Pan!"

"Ganny Pan loves you, my Dickon," his grandmother responded, lifting him up to settle on her hip.

Something went click in Tamzin's mind.

Nanny Lu loves you, my Zandie.

"Bleddy hell! Now I have one more thing to tell you!" she exclaimed.

Eleven interested faces turned her way.

"Eh?" Lars said.

Tamzin cast a guilty look at Matin. "I meant to tell you about things first, but what with everything else it went out of my mind."

Misty said, "Don't leave us in suspense, sweeting. And Lars, do stop flying up into the boughs over a little confidence between sisters-to-be. Otherwise, I might be compelled to tell her about the cream and honey and a particularly venturesome wasp."

"All right!" Tamzin raised her voice to get their attention. She began ticking items off on her fingers. "First thing! Tomorrow, Matin and I are welcoming a pup called Shoe into our lives. She's Fou's daughter, and he picked her out of the litter today."

She glanced at Matin and found him smiling at her. "Shoe?"

"She's our wedding present from Daylight and Garret."

"I hope she gets along with our wedding present from Misty and Lars," Matin said equably.

"They're giving us Dickon?"

This was pure provocation, and sure enough, Misty conjured a small sponge cake from somewhere and threw it at Tamzin.

"No, sweeting. Dickon is all ours for now—although you are welcome to borrow him sometimes."

"Thank you." Tamzin wiped the cream off her face and absently sucked her fingers.

"It's a pony," Lars said. He conjured a warm cloth and Tamzin completed her clean up and tossed it back.

She clasped her hands. "Oh, how wonderful! One of the miniatures?"

"Yes. A skewbald filly out of Painted Lady by Trumpet Voluntary. You can have a riding horse too—just say the word. You can keep it *over here* or at the stables, but a mini can live with you."

A mini pony would be perfect to draw as an illustration for Emily's book, and Tamzin clapped her hands in delight. She smiled at Matin. "You can name this one, unless she has a name already."

"I already did," he said.

"Oh?"

"Hush. She's a chatty little beast and I foresee us saying her name rather a lot. She likes dogs, fortunately."

"What else?" Nessa asked.

"Okay. Second thing! I found my way back to the shop where I got my green dress. It's called *Fairings,* and it's run by Matin's friend Otto's mother."

"Oh, I know it! Lovely place. I bought a dress there to wear to Misty and Lars' wedding," Matin's mother, Lirrin, said.

Her husband, Bay, shot her a look which made Tamzin think that dress must have been something special. He was very much like his sons, which made Tamzin disposed to enjoy his company.

Tamzin took a deep breath. "Third thing! I ordered my wedding dress while I was there. It can be ready in about two weeks' time."

"Perfect. You can be a June bride," Lirrin said. She added, "I'll have to go shopping again. And Bay, you may not come unless you promise to stay out of the changeroom."

Matin said, "Did you order me some wedding clothes too, my managing maid?"

"I don't know what elf men wear to get married in — unless what Garret wore when he married Daylight is standard?"

"Lend you some britches, man," one of the godbrothers said.

"Wid an extra layer at the front for dacency," the other added.

Matin said, "Why are you two still here? Haven't you got poteen to brew, or colleens to court?"

"You'll need a come-to-me," the other godbrother said. "I'll be off to make it."

"Just who is getting married, here?" Matin asked.

"You are, man, but no elf can fashion a come-to-me properly. It takes a man o' the green way to do it right."

"Do I get to have one too?" Tamzin asked.

To her consternation, Ronan and Faolin both turned to stare at her.

"What's wrong?"

"Sure, darlin', you have one already!"

"What? Oh! That's right. Tiernan gave me one from Nuala." Tamzin clapped her hand to her chest, before recalling it was pinned to the dress she'd been wearing earlier.

The godbrothers shook their heads in unison. "No, the one from our godbrother here—" Ronan indicated Matin.

"You mean my lovely dolphin? Or my bracelet?"

"No—the one ye've had this long time."

"I give up. I thought I spoke gossoon pretty well, but I have no idea what you two are talking about."

One of the brothers pointed at her shoes. "Sure, can't ye see it shinin' bright as his love for ye?"

Tamzin felt a hot blush surge up her face. *Surely*, they didn't mean the orris stone pendant she kept in her spy-heel. That had nothing to do with Matin. It had been a gift for her first love, Dequan, and one day she would give it to him.

No, they didn't mean that. Faolin was pointing to the other shoe—the one whose heel didn't open.

Tamzin looked enquiringly at Matin. His face, usually fair-skinned, had gone a dull red. "Matin? Do *you* know what these two are talking about?"

Matin sighed.

"Do I have to put a compulsion on you to tell?"

That brought everyone to attention. "You can't—can you?" Nessa asked.

"Not a fay one, no, but I have my ways . . ." She slowly tied a knot in the air and made a twisting motion beneath it.

Matin said, hastily, "Have a look inside that second heel."

48

"It won't open for me."

"It will once he conjures it," Misty put in.

Of course. She used to have these shoes.

Tamzin removed her shoes. She checked the familiar heel that still contained the orris stone pendant, wrapped in a scrap of galleonfee cloth to prevent it from rattling about. The heel had once contained Matin's telephone number, a wad of chewing gum, and an emergency fifty dollar note. Now, there was only the stone.

She swivelled the heel closed on those memories.

She then laid hold of the second heel but, as ever, it seemed immoveable.

She looked up at Misty, who said, "Matin, undo whatever you did to that shoe *at once*."

Matin lifted his hand and made a twist in the air. "Now try."

Tamzin obeyed and this time, the heel clicked aside, just as the other had.

Inside, she saw another wad of gum, now desiccated and chalky with age. It secured a small object wrapped in two layers of paper. She unwrapped the outer layer and when she read the pencilled words, they plucked at her memory.

If you come to me, don't you think I'll love you, and warm you, and do whatever I can to make you smile?

That's almost what he said to me that day . . .

She kissed the paper and laid it aside before investigating the second layer. This one was blank, and inside was a plain gold ring.

Tamzin stared at it.

"This was my great-great-grandmother's," Matin said quietly. "I only just remember her. She went to glory when I wasn't much older than Dickon. She left this ring with Mum, to give to me when I got enough years. Mum, what did she say?"

"For the morning boy to give to his beloved," Lirrin

quoted. "She left something for all her descendants for the next several generations, but this one was her wedding ring. It's made of island gold because her man came from the Star Pin."

"I had *his* ring, for the happy girl to give to her beloved," Misty said.

Lars raised a large hand, displaying a gold ring made with a twist. "This one."

"Misty was always such a happy baby, we knew right away," Bay said.

"And I have this—" Olivier clicked his fingers and conjured an earring set with a sparkling red stone. "For the lad who loves the silver one." He held it out to Nessa. "It's white gold, not silver, but maybe you could wear it as a pin?"

Nessa's bright eyes flooded with sudden tears.

"My great-grandmother was a remarkable woman," Lirrin said. "She left a chest of trinkets, and whenever a new child is born into the family, we look for a description and match it up. Obviously, Olivier and Misty weren't born when she passed into glory, let alone Dickon, but she seemed to know."

"And you gave this to *me*?" Tamzin said.

Matin nodded. "We always give them to someone else."

"But—you had no idea if you'd ever see me again!"

"Of course he did, darlin'," Ronan said.

"Is it not a come-to-me?" his brother added.

"Niver fails. And ye've been dancin' on love all this time."

"I was going to give it to you on our wedding day if it hadn't come to light before then," Matin said, looking bashful.

"Well then!" Tamzin kissed the ring and returned it to its hiding place. "We'll take it out then, as you planned."

"In two weeks' time," Matin said.

"Yes. In two weeks, I'll be yours officially, although it seems to me I've been yours for a long time already—dancing with your love, although I didn't always know it."

Silence ensued for a while, until Tamzin suddenly remembered the other thing she had to tell Matin. But that could wait a while, because she had to work out what it meant to her.

CHAPTER SIX: RAINBOWS

Tamzin Herrick, June, 2020

Tamzin's wedding dress was everything she hoped.

When she went for her fitting, *Fairings* was crowded with her friends, who had arrived by her invitation. Gillan St Ives came, standing in for the mother of the bride. Unexpectedly, she brought Daylight, with whom she had struck up an unlikely friendship now there was no risk of the halfling accountant beguiling either of Gillan's sons. The Dames with Dogs were represented by Florida and Nell, who carried her chihuahua, Pepe, in his sling. Lirrin and Misty came with Nessa and Mim, and Annie Blue joined them unexpectedly after spotting them from across the road where she'd been buying running shoes.

Tamzin had determinedly thought of Dequan's ex-girlfriend as a client, but Annie was convinced they were friends, so she had recently decided she might as well accept Annie's definition. As Matin had once pointed out, they had a fair bit in common, including their taste in men. Annie had fancied him at one point, when she had thought he was nothing more personal than Tamzin's neighbour. She was, as Matin had stated, a decent woman, and so she had backed away from anything more than civility with him.

Tamzin looked around the smiling women, all of whom wished her well without reservation. There were missing faces, to be sure. She couldn't have all the Dames. She would have loved to invite Pen Inkersoll, but Pen lived a long way down the coast of Victoria, where she did her illustrative work and sometimes helped her husband with his investigation business — Inkersolve. She had no idea where Jordana Dane was, though she was sure she'd have had her baby by now. Most of all, she thought of Emily, and the friendship they were healing with patience and acceptance.

Emily should *be here. She's my oldest friend.*

She did the next best thing, keying Emily's number into her phone and flipping it into Face-to-Face mode when she answered.

"Tamzin!" Emily sounded startled but pleased to hear from her.

"I wanted to show you my wedding dress," Tamzin said. She handed the phone to Annie who, as one of the younger humans present, capably backed away to get Tamzin in shot and on speaker.

Emily said, sedately, "You look magical, Tamzin. I got married in the whole champagne lace and tulle shebang. It was what Jamie and I both wanted, but I see that wouldn't suit you." She added wistfully, "I wish I was the sort of person who wore shifting rainbows."

To Tamzin's bemusement, Lirrin, Gillan, Daylight, and Jacaranda all reacted to this statement, flinching or lifting a finger as if listening for a whisper.

What?

Oh, right, Emily made a wish in the hearing of a bunch of fairies . . . that means there is a shifting rainbow somewhere in Emily's future.

She beckoned for Annie to bring the phone back. "Emily, you *are* that sort of person. Your Jacaranda Journey story is going to bring rainbows into so many readers' lives."

"*Our* story," her old friend said. "Tamzin and Emily forever, right?" She smiled, and the screen went blank.

Daylight said, "So that's why you looked so shifty when I told you we'd be forever friends. You had one already — until you didn't."

"It's complicated," Tamzin said.

She turned to see herself in the wide mirror Jacaranda provided for her clients. She lifted her skirts to see the perfect match with her shoes.

"What are you doing with your hair?" Jacaranda asked.

"Half-up?" Tamzin hazarded.

"Luce, would you?"

Jacaranda gestured to her assistant, whose gentle hands gathered Tamzin's hair into a neat twist.

"You probably need earrings to pull that off," Jacaranda said.

A customer who had just stepped into the shop turned to glance at them. "Maybe something like these," she suggested.

Tamzin looked at her, seeing an Indian print skirt, a ruffled blouse, sandals and wavy brown hair, going grey at the temples.

The woman stepped forward with a light step, as if she were waltzing to unheard music. She unhooked gold hoops from her ears and offered them on her palm.

Tamzin stared at her. "*Mummy*?"

"Dearest Abbie-Ballerina. But you look like a fairy woman now." She nodded to Jacaranda's assistant. "If it isn't Lu Ellington, the nanny from boo-boo land. No, don't look so scared, woman. For what it's worth, I'm sorry we reacted so badly when Alexandra got hurt. She had a shocking temper, and she probably threw herself out of your arms and brought it on herself. No great harm done, but I still wouldn't recommend you as nanny of the year. Nannies that are sacked ought not to keep coming to work, don't you agree? I hope you're having a happy life, though."

She waved her hand to attract Tamzin's attention. "It would be nice if you could wear these earrings at your wedding. Your dad and I chose them together, way back then, when we were setting up as Ashley and Mac, so they're a gift from both of us."

Tamzin held out her hand. She would *not* ask how Mummy came to be here. She said, "Thank you. Would you come to our wedding?"

Ada looked tempted. "I would like to, but after what your elf man did to Wayne, I think Hugh wants to stay well clear of him."

"Hugh?"

"Yes, and by the way, I'm Agatha—Shakespeare."

"Bleddy hell!" Tamzin said.

Ada inclined her head. "I'll take this, please, just in case I change my mind about the wedding," she said to Jacaranda, whisking a frilled blouse from a rack, seemingly at random.

Jacaranda went to ring it up.

Tamzin examined the earrings, "Nanny Lu, would you hold these up for me? My ears aren't pierced, so I'll have to get them adapted as hook-overs."

The door closed behind Ada.

Florida said, "That was Breezy—right? My God, I'd *never* have picked her."

"No . . . well, that's the way she looked when she was Mummy . . . Ashley Stevenson. Older, of course. However, she seems to be Agatha Shakespeare now, so if you see her again, she'll look different. Maybe like a librarian."

"And she didn't ask after Fou," Florida said, frowning. "The nerve of the woman!"

Annie said, "Whatever is going on? Who was she? Why did she call you Abbie? Who's Wayne? And what elf man have you got, and what did he do to Wayne?"

Tamzin said, "It's such a very, very long story, Annie. You probably won't believe it, but remind me to tell you some-time, preferably *after* the wedding."

Chapter Seven: A June Wedding

Tamzin Campania, June, 2020

Tamzin and Matin's wedding was held in the Open Chapel in the Fairy Gardens at Windhill.

Caddy Hildebrand, the first Dame Tamzin had met, suggested the venue, on the grounds that a chapel was more holy than the Dames' club house, but less formal than most churches. Not only that, but the gardens, with their groves and bowers, grottos and vistas, and quaint winding paths, allowed for a great many attendees who couldn't be fitted on an official guest list.

The Dames did the catering, with great cauldrons of soup, and platters of bread, fruit and cakes.

The Dames even provided a celebrant in the motherly person of Reverie Eden who had been ordained three years before, mainly, as she put it, to ease her friends gently into matrimony.

Daylight seemed miffed that the Dames had a parson, and that she hadn't known.

"Her Dame Name is Rev," Tamzin pointed out.

"Yes—but her first name is Reverie, so she's Rev Rev Eden. Sneaky."

Tamzin spent her last night as Tamzin Herrick at her beloved Fiddler's Rest, with her dogs Fou and Shoe breathing quietly in their baskets beside her.

Matin's aunt—or maybe more of a cousin—Merimbula was singing duets in the spare room with her friend Costas, accompanied by her spinet and Costas' lyre, and Tamzin found the music soothing.

Olivier and Nessa planned to move into the main bedroom the next day, so Tamzin felt that her beloved home would be in good hands.

In the morning, Gillan and Daylight arrived for breakfast, and Gillan drove Tamzin to Windhill.

"I'm sorry your mother won't be here," Gillan said abruptly.

Tamzin, already arrayed in her magical rainbow gown, said placidly, "For all I know, she might be! After all, Breezy and Clem were Dames for a couple of years, and they might still have some lines of communication. Just look out for a woman in a frilled blouse from *Fairings.* But whether she shows up or not, you're the one I want making sure I don't have my skirts tucked into my knickers. You and Bran and the boys have always had my back."

"I wish—" Gillan began.

"No, you don't. You're delighted with Githa and Morgana. They're pisky perfection."

"I know." Gill put away her melancholy and said, "I hope Bran's behaving. He was having a glass of poteen with some of the other men at the club before driving on to the Gardens. They don't usually serve it there, but someone gifted them with some—"

Tamzin had a good idea of who that *someone* might be. The godbrothers had a high opinion of their brewing and distilling capabilities and a fascination with weddings.

She said, "He'll be fine. Everything will be fine. It wouldn't dare be otherwise."

Gillan pulled up outside the gate to the Gardens. One of the features of the place was that it was foot-traffic only.

Many of the guests had already arrived, but Tamzin spotted one young elf man she didn't know. He had darker hair than most, and he was measuring the gates.

"Don't mind me," he said, stepping aside to let them pass. He smelled strongly and pleasantly of marmalade.

"Are you here for the wedding, master?" Gillan asked.

"I didn't know there was one until people started showing up. I'm a sculptor. I'm doing some giant statues to act as guardians for the gates."

"They're statues of my parents," Caddy Hildebrand said, gliding up beside them with her dog, Mary-Mary, at her side. "Have you finished measuring, Xavier?"

"Just about. Who's getting married? No one's said."

"Elfie, here, is wedding Matin Campania," Caddy told him.

"Don't know him—but good luck anyway," he said. "Getting married myself next year, I hope." He nodded to Caddy. "I'll be in touch about the dimensions soon."

"Can someone keep an eye on Shoe?" Tamzin asked, detaching her puppy from the hem of her dress.

"I'll keep her out of trouble," Daylight said. "Fou, too, and his bear." She took charge of the dogs. "I left Shelley and Atapeke with Mama Rosebay. I do hope she survives the Atapeke."

Tamzin, walking along a path bordered by hellebore and scented with winter-flowering buddleia and wintersweet, reflected that it was more like a giant picnic than a wedding. Her heart sang.

She spotted Misty and Lars bouncing Dickon along between them. Next came Matin's parents with Olivier and Nessa, Aunt Mim and Costas. They all, including Costas, hugged her in greeting. She bounced off Costas' small paunch, which made him roar with laughter.

"Where's Matin?" she asked.

The family exchanged glances. "We thought *you* had him," Misty said.

Daylight said, "He and Gar went off somewhere a while ago, but Gar swore and declared he'd have him here in time."

"They'd better hurry then," Gillan said. "A bride may be late for her wedding, but not the groom."

Tamzin spotted Annie Blue, deep in conversation with a brown-haired young man she didn't recognise, and the St Ives brothers with their betrotheds. There was Otto Fairling, arm in arm with two shapely young women in blue. They looked mischievous and sensible, and she thought that was a perfect combination for Otto. *Keep him on his toes.*

Branok stepped out of the shadows and said, "Gill, there are four leprechauns here — how the hell did that happen?"

"Matin's godfather, *his* father, and two of the godbrothers, representing the whole tribe," Tamzin said. "They're supposed to be glamoured. Can someone . . ."

"I don't expect anyone will notice in this crowd," Gillan said.

"I did."

"But you're observant, and you know what you're looking at."

They reached the open chapel, which the Dames had decorated with boughs of wintersweet and acacia. Reverie Eden was there in a cassock, with her spaniel, Debussy, beside her.

Otto had moved over to a sound system, and Tamzin heard some of her own fiddle music playing softly.

That was lovely, but —

There was Nell with Pepe *and* Brian.

Nell said cheerfully, "Pity we couldn't get a command performance from *Courtesan.*"

"We'll see them at Winterwatch next month," Tamzin reminded.

Reverie had set up her lectern and was looking enquiringly about.

"There you are Elfie!" she said. "You look delightful —

rainbows are promises."

"You won't forget my name's really Tamzin, will you?" Tamzin said.

"So it is. Better make a note of that. Where's Matin?"

"Darned if I know," Gillan said. "Daylight's man is supposed to be keeping tabs on him."

Mull St Ives came up and kissed Tamzin on the cheek. "Good morning, my sister. You look good enough to put in a vase. Don't worry about your man. He's just pulled up alongside the gates with Daylight's elf. Got a woman with them. She looks a bit flustered—I'll go and take charge of her so Matt can get organised."

He took off at a run and returned shortly after with a young woman in a blue skirt. Her shawl danced with shifting colours.

"Emily!" Tamzin pounced on her. "How ever did you get here?"

"You did invite me," Emily said.

"Yes, but I never thought you'd be able to come at such short notice."

"Neither did I, but—I got a message to meet Matin at the pub and—God, I can't believe I'm saying this. I just *don't* go to pubs to meet strange men, but I thought he might be bringing a message from you. Pop approved of him, anyway. The barmaid said he was waiting in the scullery and—"

"And he brought you here through the gate. And I don't suppose he had time to debrief you or disclose to you or anything."

Daylight, still armed with the dogs, came up. Her small baby bump showed proudly through a tight-fitting dress of bright yellow velvet. "Hello, Emily. I saw you on Tamzin's phone the day she had the fitting, and I have a set of your books. Tamzin gave them to Daffodil for a pre-birthday present, but I read them already. I love kids' books and yours have a zing to them."

Emily looked bewildered.

"Sorry, forgot you don't know me. I'm one of Tamzdie's friends, Dahlia Rosebay. I'm married to Matin's friend, Garret, and I'm looking after their dogs while they get married. How about you come and stand with us, and I'll explain everything to you *after* the wedding. You can hold Shoe."

Emily smiled tentatively.

Tamzin hugged her. "It's so good to see you! I have some more Jacaranda Journey pictures to show you—"

"And now I know a bit more about—"

Matin ran up, and Gillan said, "Great bogle!" and grabbed his arm. "Get over there, idiot boy, or Tamzin will get tired of waiting and marry someone else! I'm sure there would be plenty of volunteers."

Emily flung up her hands, laughing. "Oh, *Tamzin*, this is all so mad—and *this* is your friend Dahlia!"

"You don't know the half of it," Daylight said with relish. "Come with me and we'll be part of the loving line. Afterwards, you can tell me what you and Tam got up to when she was being Jade. I know you're best friends forever, and so you and I will be too, by association . . ."

The loving what?

Branok St Ives took Tamzin's arm as the fiddle music switched into *Damhsa Bainise*, the wedding dance Tamzin had played at Shay's wedding to Honorée, and at the ball on the night of the pink pavilion. She had not played it for Cornelius and Briar, because she'd been away at Balla Cloiche by then. She hoped Master Treelove had done the honours. After all, he had taught it to her.

It was bizarre, walking arm in arm with her solicitor between lines of her friends all to the joyous sound of her own playing, but it was also *right*. She had always loved leprechaun music ever since . . .

Oh, ever since Geenie played for Zandie and Nanny Lu.

Branok stopped by the altar and kissed her on the brow. "Be happy, always, daughter of my heart."

"I shall be!"

He handed her over to Matin, who smiled at her.

"Greet you, my darling dolphin."

"Greet you, my beautiful elf man," she responded.

Reverie Eden said, "Bless you two who have come to be married and bless the friends and loved ones who have come to stand as witness. Bless the ones who bring music, and food, flowers, and love, and bless whatever little beastie is gnawing on my shoe."

Daylight muttered something to Emily.

Emily made a grab for Shoe, who growled in puppy protest. "Sorry, I was distracted, and she escaped to the length of the leash," she said.

Reverie Eden gave her a beatific smile. "Pups do that!" She waited for a few seconds while Emily settled her charge against her rainbow shawl.

"We are gathered . . ."

The service went on as Tamzin Elfie Herrick and Matin Bell Campania were given into one another's keeping. There was a brief pause while Tamzin removed her shoe and Matin retrieved the ring it had guarded for so long.

In turn, she gave him one that Aureate Shale had made, and which she had been wearing against her heart for the past ten days as they prepared for a hasty wedding.

After they exchanged the most sedate kiss of their lives so far, the minister asked for everyone to welcome Matin and Tamzin Campania.

Some hours later, Tamzin Campania stood in the bedroom of Delphinium House.

Fou, Shoe and the chatty pony, Hush, were being cared for by Misty and Lars for the night. Daylight had volunteered to see Emily safely back to the Harvest Hob, and to debrief her over a shandy.

"And don't worry, in view of Daffodil's quarter or so human blood, *I* shall be drinking cherry juice."

My two forever friends . . .

Matin gently unhooked the gold hoop earrings from Tamzin's ears.

"I hope you're not too disappointed that your parents didn't show."

She smiled at him. "I never expected them to, and I don't mind a bit, and I'm not absolutely sure they didn't . . . there were plenty of strangers pottering about. Maybe they were the two ladies with bustles, parasols and picture hats."

He still looked solemn, so she added, "You're my family now. Anyway, I expect they'll show up again sometime, with or without parasols. Ada looked a bit tempted when I mentioned grandchildren, so one day we might get a visit from Adeline Burns. Not sure about Guy Herrick, though."

He kissed her neck as he undid the rainbow gown.

"You're not conjuring," Tamzin observed as she untoggled his shirt.

"Too nervous," he said.

"Oh, so that's why we had to get the ring out of my shoe by hand. I was expecting it to magically appear."

"That, and because there were undisclosed-to humans in the crowd."

He lifted off the green slip that went under the dress.

Tamzin sat to remove her spy-heeled shoes. She took off her bodice and knickers, then got into their brand-new bed.

Matin finished stripping and got in beside her. They rolled in to meet one another.

"So, Master Campania, we're going to have a go at planting our baby tonight," Tamzin said.

"We are."

"I know what we said, but do you mind *very* much if it

doesn't involve commands or roaring? All that is wonderful, but I thought maybe we could do that *first*, and do the planting on round two. Would that be all right with you?"

"Anything is all right with me," he said, putting his arms around her.

Tamzin kissed him, and she snuggled close. She raised a hand to deliver a swat, but then she lowered it again. rolled onto her back. "Make love to me?"

He kissed her, and they came together in a tangle of legs.

"Matin?"

"Yes?" He shifted and she gasped with pleasure.

"Never mind round two. Let's do it now. Don't hold. Just let it happen . . ."

"I couldn't hold if I wanted to," he said.

"Can we call her Music?"

His arms tightened.

She gasped again.

"Greet you, Music!" he said. Then he *gave.*

PART TWO: NELIS

CHAPTER EIGHT: NELIS AND XAVIER

Nelis Winter, Sydney, Christmas Eve, 2020

Nelis and Xavier had enjoyed a busy day. They'd begun with a good deal of noisy sex in their bedroom. Nelis had expected that, since Xavier Partridge was an elf man under the Christmas Hot, but she hadn't expected it to be quite so intense.

After all, it wasn't their first time.

She'd been unaware that the Hot existed when she first kissed Xavier at their school leavers' dinner. It was a prank gone wrong, but the kiss rapidly escalated as her marmalade-smelling schoolmate, always so gawky, and so sweet, had suddenly turned seductive.

Nelis, though bewildered, had found herself more than willing to do whatever he wanted. She'd had a thing about him anyway, and every nerve was zinging with what she assumed was passion.

She *wanted* him, on her, under her, in her — any way he chose.

She was almost feverish with desire when he suddenly paused and asked her, oddly, if she *had enough years*. What? He rephrased it. Was she his age, eighteen?

No, she was seventeen, but it was absolutely fine.

Only, according to Xavier, it absolutely wasn't. He bolted, leaving Nelis shamed, miserable, and with nothing to do but sob her embarrassment out in the ladies' loo.

Lucy Tan had rescued her, and she'd never seen Xavier

again until—well, until a year ago today, when *his* cousin Niall and *her* new friend Frances invited the pair of them to a Christmas Eve party.

Later, Nelis thought Niall should have known better. He was an elf man, after all, so what the hell was he doing inviting other elves to a party on Christmas Eve?

Nelis and Xavier had never made it there, anyway, as a stop at the *Pear Tree* pub had led to Xavier telling Nelis he was an elf, which led to Nelis making a run for it, only to fetch up in the middle of an elf orgy in the back bar of the pub. The barmaid had fed her a concoction called salviation to calm her down, but Nelis was human . . . and it hadn't worked.

Xavier had rescued her and put her to bed in an upstairs room. In the early hours, the effect of the salviation had worn off, and Nelis, now in her right mind, had finally settled her unfinished business with Xavier.

It had been hot, delicious, and wildly fulfilling, and when they discovered the party had been put on hold because Frances' cousin had gone into labour, they'd returned to the *Pear Tree* for some more hot action.

They'd been a couple ever since.

So, that was the Hot, and she'd been more than up for it this year. She and Xavier were in love, and engaged, and Nelis couldn't wait for the Hot to hit.

It hadn't been the way either of them had expected, but they'd worked it out. That was what they always did these days when things went unexpected. They worked it out.

The next stop of the day was breakfast at the *Dark Room* café with their old friend Lucy Tan, she who had soothed Xavier and rescued Nelis on the long-ago night of their leavers' dinner debacle.

Lucy had been having adventures as well, and she was gloriously pregnant to her lover, Paris, with whom she planned to spend Christmas *over there* in the fay homeland.

The only dark spot in Lucy's joy, aside from a bit of parental disapproval, was that she felt bad about abandoning her cousin Dequan, who had hoped to spend Christmas with her as usual.

Instead, he had gone off alone on a mystery holiday with the *Vouch-Safe* company for which Lucy worked.

He'd gone alone because not only was Lucy otherwise engaged, but Dequan had just broken up with his girlfriend, Puck.

Dequan Qin, handsome, personable, capable and kind, had no trouble finding lovely girlfriends, but, in Lucy's words, he never seemed able to commit to a relationship. Lucy blamed this on what had happened to him back in his last year of school. He had gone to the formal with his girlfriend Tamzin Herrick, and they had danced and kissed and parted with the understanding that they'd spend summer together, and as soon as Tamzin turned eighteen, they'd become an official couple.

Dequan had a beautiful Christmas present for Tamzin, and she'd had something for him, but the gifts had never been exchanged. Lucy knew Dequan's gift to Tamzin was still in his curio cabinet. Where hers to him was, no one knew, because Tamzin had disappeared.

Her family had moved away the day after the formal. and in all the years since, Dequan had never been able to find her.

Lucy therefore wanted to know if Nelis and Xavier had any idea on what had happened to Tamzin.

Unfortunately, they didn't. Xavier had never known her, and though Nelis remembered her as a pretty girl with wavy hair, she hadn't seen her in over a decade.

She sympathised with Dequan, whom she knew slightly, and with Lucy, who felt bad about putting herself ahead of her cousin, but they all agreed there was nothing to be done.

With breakfast over, and Lucy departed to her lover,

Xavier and Nelis went to enjoy the Windhill Fairy Gardens, where Xavier had shown her the super-life-size statues he'd made of the founders, Jacobi and Barbara le Fay. They wandered through the gardens and discussed plans, including a journey on the galleon fleet that sailed perpetually *over there*. Nelis thought such a thing sounded bizarre, but Xavier, as an elf, saw nothing odd about taking leave of absence from their work and spending an extended time in fairyland. Nelis agreed it would be fun, but she stipulated they would *not* vanish as Tamzin Herrick had done, and in any case, they wouldn't leave until well after their upcoming February wedding.

Next New Year's Eve, they agreed.

It seemed comfortably far away.

They stood on a sandstone outcrop, looking out over the small bay.

Xavier had suggested they might take one of the boats out, but Nelis was hanging back a bit.

"What if the Hot comes in again? If it happens here, we could get down into the bushes, or — I don't know — "

She knew once the imperative struck, Xavier would be desperate for her to take him. She'd want him too, but the idea of sex in public, in a wildly rocking small boat, made her nervous.

"I'm fine, now." He squeezed her hand.

"We thought you were fine when we left home, but it came in again at the *Dark Room.*"

"That's what the suite's for."

Flick Dark, the co-owner of the *Dark Room*, was an elf halfling, so naturally she made provision for any elf couple who needed urgent privacy over Christmas. Her husband was human, so she understood some of the difficulties faced by other mixed couples.

"I know, but there's no suite here," Nelis said.

"I'm all right now, Nelis." Xavier's voice was steady.

"You thought—"

"I'm all right now because you solved the problem in the suite. The Hot was worse because you're human and I was worried about you."

"Rather than concentrating on getting your rocks off in spectacular elf fashion," she said.

"I suppose it's like being with someone with a peanut allergy. You could never quite relax into a party because you'd be afraid of the food."

"So, now I'm a peanut allergicist," she grumbled.

"No, *I* am. You're not the one with the exploding cock."

"Oh yes I am!" They were facing out to the deserted bay, so she felt safe to put her hand against the front of his pants. She pressed gently. "Oh-oh. You're hard."

Xavier removed her hand from his pants and kissed her palm. "That's just normal. Not the Hot."

"Normal?"

"I'm standing here in a beautiful place with my favourite person, we're talking about sex, and she's just touching me the way she does when she wants—"

"Less of the *she*," Nelis growled. She turned to face him. "Can you cast a glamour?"

"Yes, but I can wait." He leaned in and kissed her.

"What if *I* can't?"

"I think we both need to wait—unless you want to skip the orgy and go right home."

Nelis said, "I am determined to go to that orgy. I want to enjoy it, the way I couldn't last year. I also want to get together with Otto and the girls—"

"And learn their double-handling technique. I know. You said."

"And we need to go early."

Xavier glanced at the angle of the sun. "We have plenty of

time to take the boat out."

"All right. But if you have a problem, don't just suffer."

They walked down the winding path to the small cove, where Xavier untied one of the small sailboats. "No wind, so we'll use the motor," he said.

Nelis climbed in, and sat on the forward seat, feeling the gentle pitch of the boat as Xavier pushed it out and jumped on board. They puttered out in the blue and Xavier cut the motor. They sat in silence, watching the horizon sway.

"This is beautiful," Nelis said.

"It is—"

"It's a lovely day."

"And not over yet. We have the orgy—if you insist—and after that comes Frances and Niall's party."

"Let's hope no one has an inconveniently timed baby this year."

"I don't think anyone is due. Frances and Niall have six months to go, Kendy and Piers—no. Flick and Chas are obviously not expecting. Eve and Raph—no idea."

"That's that then, unless Frances has found someone new to invite."

"You never know, with Frances," he agreed.

"Xav, why *do* they have their party on Christmas Eve? It's a bit risky, with—let's see—you and Niall being elves and Flick, Piers and Eve halflings."

Xavier said, "I'm the only one likely to do anything untoward. Niall's a Christmas elf, and the others are maids –aside from Piers who threw hard to his courtfolk side. Midsummer is *his* trigger."

"I can't pretend to understand that."

"I don't either. None of us do, properly, other than Piers and Kendy. Piers is writing a series of books."

"About the Hot?"

"Presumably that's covered, but not blow by blow. It's

called *Orders of the Fay*. I'll get you a set for your birthday."

Nelis nodded drowsily. She'd had a busy night and she supposed the one ahead would be busy too.

"What should I wear?"

"Your pink party dress."

"No, I mean to the orgy."

"Something comfortable."

"You're no help."

"You're going to be taking it off, anyway," he pointed out.

"What—right off? Can't I just lift my skirts?"

"The others will be mostly stripped down."

"Grete won't."

"She doesn't participate."

Nelis smiled. "Grete is not going to be pleased to see me. Maybe I'll get lucky and someone else will be on duty."

Xavier reached over towards the engine switch.

"What are you doing?"

"If we're going to talk, we might as well go back inshore."

She put her hand on his arm. "Let's just sit here a while, and—"

"Kiss," he said.

"Perfect."

Chapter Nine: The Orgy

Nelis Winter, Sydney, Christmas Eve, 2020

N elis woke when Xavier put a gentle hand on hers. "Hmm?"

"Time to go. In fact, we're running a bit late, so I think we'll need to go as we are."

"That's all right," she said. After all, her full-skirted dress was clean and comfortable. Xavier could conjure them into fresh clothing, but it didn't seem worth asking.

They returned to shore and stowed the boat. Then they walked back through the gardens, bypassing the chapel where Xavier had seen a rainbow bride back in June.

Nelis thought about her wedding dress. Her childhood and much of her teens had been spent in homespun, recycled, re-purposed clothing because that was the way her dad, Snow-land Winter, liked it. Her mum, Daisy Comice, had gone along with it, but once Snow had departed for a long-term project overseas, Daisy and Nelis had moved out of the eco-cabin and acquainted themselves with convenience foods. Daisy had acquired a love affair with the shopping channel. They had soon calmed down. Snow was still away, but he and Daisy got together at regular intervals. Snow had even met Xavier, and the meeting had gone far better than Nelis had feared. Xavier, after all, lived part of the time *over there* where electricity didn't work.

The pink party dress she wore to her class leavers' dinner had been bought as an act of rebellion soon after Snow's departure, but Xavier had liked it, and he liked its successor, which was also pink, but shorter.

One good thing about elves, Nelis reflected, was that they were never bothered about saying what they liked. Xavier *liked* pink silk with ruffles, especially when it encased his bride-to-be.

Nelis had asked Xavier what elves wore to their weddings, and he'd just said she could have whatever she liked. She'd gone on to ask Flick, who said she'd married Chas in a white mini with slashed sleeves, decorated with tinsel, and Frances, who said she rather thought she'd married Niall in a sheet.

"What on earth for?"

Frances had widened her beautiful eyes and brushed aside her waterfall of red-gold hair with her magical left hand. "It made it quicker to start the honeymoon."

That didn't sound likely, but with Frances, one never knew.

In the end, she'd decided to enlist Daisy's help, suggesting they should shop together.

"I want you in something sparkling and slinky and extra pretty. No dowdy matronly pants suit for you," she said, and Daisy's eyes lit up.

"If Dad shows up, I expect he'll be in his handwoven eco-hair onesie, but that's fine too. In fact—I think we'll put it on the invitations that everyone is to wear their favourite thing."

"What about you?" Daisy asked.

Nelis shook her head. "I don't have a favourite thing, other than my pink party dress, and I don't want to get married in that. I want something Xav hasn't already seen and taken off me."

There was no point asking Daisy what she'd worn to her wedding, because Daisy had been never married—not even to Snow.

Daisy suggested, "What about a vintage party dress?"

"For both of us! It's a date!"

That having been decided, Nelis had stopped stressing.

Unfortunately, deciding what to get wasn't the same as getting it, and she had less than six weeks to go.

Must get hold of Mum when she gets back from being Snowed under.

Now wasn't the time to think of shopping. Now was the time to psych herself up for an orgy.

They stepped out of the Gardens between the founders' statues and made their way to where Nelis had parked her car. Xavier could drive, but he didn't like to, so it mostly fell to Nelis to play chauffeur.

The *Pear Tree* was in a quiet area of Sydney Nelis knew as Silent Park. Unless one knew it was there, it was easy to drive right past.

Anyone could go there, but in practice, it was usually fay and their guests. A glamour couldn't render the place quite invisible, but it did make it difficult to notice.

Nelis parked out on the street and locked the car. She and Xavier walked up the path between the quiet trees. Quite suddenly, there it was — the *Pear Tree*.

They entered the taproom, where Nelis had had a meltdown a year ago.

There was the Christmas tree, with its colourful wooden ornaments depicting the Twelve Days of Christmas. These were Xavier's work.

Nelis almost smiled as she remembered her panic when she'd spotted her first leprechauns, not to speak of braesiders with their odd heathered eyes. These days, she knew Dinny Spinnaker and the McDonalds pretty well.

The patrons were different today, but they glanced up as Xavier and Nelis entered.

Several of them nodded to Xavier, and one pretty girl wearing a lot of silver jewellery gave him a wide smile.

"Hi, Xav, looking for someone for the night?"

"I've found someone for life," he said.

"Good. I shall, too." She flicked her single earring, making it swing.

"Would you like a drink first?" Xavier asked Nelis.

"Something cold," she said.

Xavier nodded and approached the publican, who greeted him with a genial grin.

He came back with a glass of fruit juice over ice.

Nelis raised her glass to Master Perry behind the bar and sipped it slowly. Now they were at the pub, she was having serious second thoughts.

However, she was the one who had insisted on coming, so she wasn't about to back down. She absently ate one of the oat crackers that had come with the drink. At least the publican hadn't produced a huge platter such they'd been served with last year. Not yet, anyway.

Xavier took her empty glass. "Ready?"

"Yes."

She caught the other girl's grin as she turned to follow Xavier through the door leading to the less public part of the pub. She didn't know her, but she'd recognised her as a pisky maid, one of the less comfortable orders of the fay. Obviously, she and Xavier knew one another, but not well enough for the maid to have realised he was engaged.

Don't worry about it. Xav doesn't care if men greet you by name.

Bedfordshire. That was the upstairs area of private rooms. She and Xavier had spent the night there last year.

Maybe we should just go on up – there's a bed and a cuddling chair, and a bathroom and –

They passed the doors to the cellar and the kitchens. The signs suggested Master Perry had an odd sense of humour.

And there was the sign for *Release me,* which she'd mistaken for the exit last year.

She said suddenly, "If this bar is for elves who need partners for the Hot, why are Otto and the girls coming? They're married."

"Why are *we* coming?" Xavier asked.

"Because the girls promised to show us how they coordinate on Otto's balls."

"I suppose they're here for the same reason. To demonstrate. Or maybe they just enjoy it."

"If you really don't want to do this, we can go home," Nelis said.

Xavier squeezed her hand. "I think we should go in, now we're here. Last year you didn't get to participate."

"Neither did you."

"I wasn't intending to anyway," he pointed out. "We were on our way to a party, remember?"

He raised a hand and conjured the door to the release bar open. This was necessary because there was no handle this side.

Nelis supposed that was a good idea, intended to prevent unaccompanied humans from blundering in. Not that it had prevented her. Determined to escape what she thought was a dangerously unstable escort and a madhouse with green-faced men and mouthy women, she'd ducked through on the heels of two other people, tailgating without a second thought.

This time, she entered more decorously, hand in hand with an elf who had every right to be there.

The lamps were soft, but she could see the long low bar screening off part of the room from view and from earshot. She saw the tables and chairs. Two couples sat there, holding hands, sipping glasses of what she supposed was salviation. To elves, the sage cordial represented a clear head and an informed choice. To humans, it represented a loss of inhibition, a desire to babble inappropriately, and the loss of feeling in the lower limbs.

The barmaid, who was really an invigilator and facilitator,

looked up from polishing glasses. She was a tall, full-figured woman with a milkmaid braid.

Her name was Grete Luchsinger and Nelis had hoped she wouldn't be on duty today.

She smiled at them. "And what's your pleasure, master and mistress?" Her gaze sharpened and she said, mildly, "Please don't ask for salviation."

"I wasn't going to, and I didn't last time. You *gave* it to me," Nelis said. "Hello, Grete."

"Nelis. You are welcome to have cider or perry or verbena tea. None of those will have an unfortunate side effect."

"I'm fine, thanks. Master Perry gave me some fruit juice."

"Very well. Take your pleasure as you wish, and may you enter with hope and leave us with hope fulfilled." She smiled and opened a hatch to let them through.

It had been quiet, but the hatch allowed the sound to rise about them.

The space behind the bar, as before, was covered with mattresses and blankets, with linen sheets and coverlets. Cushions lay in heaps, and sprawled over it all lay at least two dozen bodies, mostly naked.

Being elves, they all had shiny hair, firm bodies and fine features. Some of them were kissing, some fondling, and several were in the throes of full-blown sex.

The words Nelis could hear were of appreciation, and desire, but not so much of love, for most of these folk weren't established couples.

Nelis winced. As she'd mentioned to Xavier earlier in the day, this wasn't what she wanted to see in cold blood. She trusted the come-hither in the air would soon have its effect on her.

She breathed deeply, enjoying the mixed scents of flowers, rain, fruit and wood—the *bouquet des fees.* All the elves she'd met smelled heavenly, although Xavier was the only one who smelled of marmalade. Trust him!

A soft hand touched her cheek, turning her face so she was nose to nose with a young woman with sweet eyes in a heart-shaped face. Curly dark hair hung over her shoulders.

"Greet you, pretty. Would you enjoy a soft service with me?"

"Thank you, Jessie, but no—I have someone with me."

The girl moved back a pace and laughed. "Ah, I remember you—the human maid who discomposed Otto. So you've come back to see us again."

"I'm with someone today," she said again. "Do you know if Otto and Kim and Charlotte are here?"

"Not yet, and maybe not at all, since they're wed," Jessie said.

"They said they were coming."

Jessie nodded down to the pillows. "Then I suggest you get some action while you wait."

She patted Nelis on the cheek and turned to a very young man wearing drawstring britches. "Greet you, pretty lad—first time?"

He nodded, looking anywhere but at Jessie.

"First Hot, or first time at all?"

"Both," he muttered.

"Are you uncomfortable down there?

He nodded again.

"I can help you, or you might rather have an older maid—or a lad. *No harm.* No shame. You do whatever is right for you. It's going to be wonderful."

He reached out but then withdrew his hand.

"You can touch me," Jessie said cheerfully. "I'd like that. I'm an elf and I need it just as much as you, remember."

He reached out again, and Jessie put out her hands and drew him up against her. Over his shoulder, she gave Nelis a merry glance and rolled her eyes expressively.

Nelis backed away. Jessie preferred women, she remembered, but it seemed she would make exceptions.

"Xavier?"

"Here," he said from behind her. "Shall we?"

She saw he had a folded sheet in his hand.

She nodded, and he led her down the narrow aisle between mattresses, chose a clear spot, and flung out the sheet.

He knelt, and said, "Come on, Nel."

Nelis joined him. "I thought Jessie liked girls," she said.

Xavier said, "Jessie does like girls. She likes boys too, and she's especially nice to the first-timers. For some of them, coming here is only a shade less frightening than having the deal with it alone."

Nelis glanced over to where Jessie was now kneeling, coaxing her charge to undo his britches.

Xavier stretched out with a sigh and held out his arms.

"We're still dressed."

"I know. It might be fun."

Nelis rolled against him. He felt warm and familiar, and he smelled of fresh marmalade. She put her hand on his chest and she wriggled her fingers inside his shirt.

His arms came around her, and he gently drew up her skirt.

They kissed.

Someone behind Nelis moaned and she shivered.

She felt Xavier's fingers stroking her thighs.

"Can we —" She swallowed.

Jessie said, "There, that's better, my, what a splendid willy! May I stroke it?"

The young man's breath hitched.

"Kiss me now, then, and you'll feel so much better soon."

She kissed Xavier. It hadn't been him speaking, but the excitement she had felt the year before was growing.

She pushed her hand down between them. "Shall I —"

"Whatever you like."

He was hard.

I thought the Hot was over for him.

He rubbed against her. "Whatever you like, but please . . . do it now."

She released the toggle on his pants and wrapped her hand around him, pressing.

His hands slid farther up her thighs, edging under her knickers.

"Ugh—" She pressed against his fingers.

A cry from the left interrupted her concentration. "Quick— quick—I'm—" The words ended in a scream.

"Hard," someone else cried out.

"Oh!" the young man exclaimed, and Jessie murmured praise and pleasure.

Xav's right. She's very nice with a first-timer. I hope he doesn't think it's any more than kindness.

"Now, we rest a bit. Oh, you're ready again? That's so fast! I'm ready, too. Feel. Let's try to go together this time. You lie down and I'll show you something nice."

Nelis tightened her grip rhythmically and cried out herself as the fingers tending her turned urgent.

She gasped, bucking against Xavier, who said, "Quick!"

She got to her knees, dragged down her knickers, and straddled him.

He got his hands on her breasts, kneading them through her dress.

He felt tense, so she moved gently until she felt him relax.

He rolled over, bringing her beside him and pulling up her skirt. He was breathing hard and laughing. "That was a rush—must have been Jessie's coaching."

Someone brushed her cheek, and a mildly sardonic voice said, "So you started the party without us."

Xavier spat out some of Nelis' hair and said, "Greet you, Otto."

Someone giggled.

Nelis sat up slowly. "Hello, Kim."

Kim Fairling smiled down at her. She was wearing a pale blue dress, which she pulled off over her head to reveal an athletic figure. She pushed the garment at Otto. "Deal with this, yes? Charlotte?"

Charlotte, Kim's co-wife, was also wearing blue. She stepped out of her skirt and shimmied out of a blouse. "These too." She bundled them in top of Kim's.

Otto Fairling, still fully dressed, said, "Since when am I your valet, maids?"

"Since we won the toss," Kim said demurely. She sat down beside Nelis. "Nel, I suggest you get that dress off. Things can get a bit — damp, often just from watching."

Charlotte pulled off her lacy camisole and stretched. "Here, Otto, look after this."

Kim undid her suspender belt and peeled off pale blue stockings. "Otto."

Two pairs of lacy blue knickers hit him in the chest. "Catch, Otto."

Otto sighed. He clicked his fingers, and the bundle of clothing vanished.

"Undress me, maids." He raised his arms. His wives removed his clothes slowly.

"Already up," Kim said disapprovingly. "Charlotte, you haven't been doing your duty. I thought you damped him down."

"I thought *you* did."

Otto turned to face Nelis. "Well now, mistress, if you wish to comment on my balls this time around, I suggest you do it now. They're freshly showered, and they have been lightly exercised, buffed and polished for your demonstration."

Nelis gulped. She glanced at Xavier and saw he was trying not to laugh.

She forced herself to look. "Very — um — "

"*Squidgy* was the term you used before, I think."

Kim tucked her arm around him. "Stop teasing the poor maid, Otto. She was under salviation, and it clarified her a bit too much. Shuffle up, Xav — Otto has to lie down so we can demonstrate our patented technique. If we do it with him standing, his knees give way, and he might fall on someone."

Xavier moved over, and Otto settled on his back with his hands behind his head.

"Watch carefully," Kim said to Nelis.

"You too, Xav," Charlotte said. "You might find it instructive." She tapped her husband's hip. "Open up."

Otto spread his legs.

Kim said, "Observe." She laid three fingers on Otto's balls and stroked them gently.

Charlotte added three of hers, stroking behind Kim's.

Kim brought her second hand into play, and Charlotte followed suit.

Nelis tried to focus on the movements as they grew faster and faster.

"Great bogle," Xavier muttered.

Otto's hips lifted.

"Down." Kim somehow got her knee on his thigh.

"Keep it up, Char," she encouraged.

Otto's head moved as if his supporting hands had clenched. "Maids . . ."

"This is where we really need a third person," Kim remarked conversationally.

"Maids!"

"Yes, a third person, to give that cock some attention. It looks — "

"Speed up a bit and we might be able to fit it in," Charlotte said.

Their stroking hands became a blur, and Otto closed his

eyes.

Nelis glanced at Xavier and saw he had done the same.

"Ten, nine," Kim began a countdown.

The stroking fingers were slapping the cock now on the up-swing, and as the countdown reached zero, both girls simultaneously stopped stroking and seized Otto's cock.

"There she blows," Charlotte said, and there it did blow.

They beamed at one another in congratulation. Charlotte patted Otto's thigh. "You held out longer than you ever did before."

"That was probably because he had an audience, and a rep to uphold," Kim said. She rubbed her hands on a piece of cloth she must have conjured. Then she turned to Nelis. "And that, Mistress Winter, is our patented double-handling technique. The secret is to give him no time at all to anticipate and no chance to move. He has to lie still and give himself into our hands."

Charlotte put her hand on her husband's lower belly. "Let's see how fast you can re-arm."

"We're not doing that again," Otto said forcefully.

"No, that was just a demo, as agreed. Any comments, Nelis?"

Nelis swallowed. "That's—extraordinary."

"We think so. If you want to have a go at Xav, we can give you some pointers. Or we could run a demo on him for you if you don't object."

Xavier said, "*I* object."

Otto tried to sit up, but Kim pushed him down. "Not yet." She said to Charlotte, "He's nearly there. Your turn."

Charlotte rubbed his thighs. "The thing is, you don't touch the target until he's nearly ready to go. See? Upstanding already, and I haven't laid so much as a fingertip on it."

Otto said, "Nelis, if your curiosity is now satisfied, maybe you could see to Xavier. I think he's about to shoot his bolt."

"You're certainly about to shoot yours, Otto," Charlotte said. "Over and easy, or shoot for the sky?"

Nelis hauled her gaze off Otto and turned to look at Xavier. "Are you okay?"

He squirmed.

Charlotte made a quick movement and was suddenly sitting on Otto and bouncing energetically. "Over easy!"

Xavier's eyes opened and bugged, and he winced. "Nelis!"

Nelis, heeding Kim's advice, stripped off her clothes. She ripped open Xavier's britches and sat on him. "If you want to look at bouncing boobs, you can look at mine," she said snappily, as if she hadn't just been entranced while watching Otto's performance.

Kim said, "Hurry up, Char—I need my turn."

"How much of that was the Hot and how much was excitement?" Nelis asked as she and Xavier left the *Pear Tree*, after a kiss on the cheek from Otto and full-bosomed hugs from his wives.

Xavier, carrying an enormous cake and a bag of fruit from Master Perry, said, "You should be able to judge for yourself. As you said, it's not what you'd want to see in cold blood, but we both managed to get in the mood."

"Everyone has such a lovely time. That shy boy that Jessie had did loosen up quickly."

"It's difficult not to, in that atmosphere," Xavier said.

"I'm not so sure about Otto. Was *he* enjoying himself? He looked a bit pained."

"Undoubtedly he was enjoying himself. He'd never have wed those two maids if he didn't enjoy being brought off that way. The chagrin was just for show."

"Kim suggested—"

"Nelis, please, let's not go into who did what to other people. I'm concerned about what *we* did. Did you enjoy it?"

"I did. I always love being with you but being among others was exciting. Seeing that boy's face when Jessie said she'd like him to touch her. Do you think she—"

"Better not to think too hard about Jessie. She's a kind maid, on the whole."

"Have *you* ever?"

Xavier said, "We can go next year if you like, and you can ask her, but I think you know the answer in that she prefers women or beginners."

"You were a beginner once."

"I was. You were there. And before you suggest you weren't there *all* the time, I'll tell you Jessie is five years younger than I am."

"Really?"

"Indeed. So while I was so far out of my depth I wasn't even trying to swim, she was blamelessly enjoying a picnic with the other youngsters too old to be minded by a Christmas sub, but too young to be concerned . . ."

Nelis pried her mind away from what wasn't her business and rested it pleasurably on something else that wasn't her business either. "Otto has beautiful balls. Almost as nice as yours."

Xavier sighed. "What *is* it with maids and balls?"

"Don't you know?"

He shook his head.

Nelis said, "Squidgy."

"Oh. Do you want to pop into the *Dark Room* to freshen up before we go to Niall and Frances?"

"Yes—as long as you can get my party dress from home. It's draped over the chair by our bed."

"I can do that."

CHAPTER TEN: A CHRISTMAS WISH

Nelis Winter, Sydney, Christmas Eve, 2020

When Nelis and Xavier reached the *Dark Room*, Flick Dark and her husband were about to close the cafe, but Flick willingly gave Nelis and Xavier leave to shower in the suite.

"I don't go to the *Pear Tree* myself, but I expect you do get sticky. Do you need to borrow some fresh knickers, Nel?"

"Xavier can get me some when he gets my dress."

"Good, but never hesitate to ask. I keep a supply of things here for anyone who needs them—tees and knickers, pullovers, and children's clothes, too. George suggested that when Joyful spilled blackberry juice all over herself one day. I wasn't here to conjure her into something fresh, but he did the best he could, bless him. He got her into one of his school shirts with a napkin around it as a belt."

George was Flick's human stepson, or son-by-love, as she referred to him. He was a dark, square-faced child who must look like his mother, since he didn't look like Flick's husband, Chas.

"George has a lot of good ideas," Flick added approvingly. "By the way, did you sort out your friend Lucy's problem?"

Nelis was unsurprised that Flick would know about that. The fay in general had excellent hearing.

"Not really. Not at all, in fact. It's one of those things no one can sort out. It involves her cousin's girlfriend who vanished years ago."

"Not a police matter?"

87

"Nothing like that. It was more like a moonlight flit. The whole family just left."

"That is odd," Flick said. She added, in an apparent change of subject, "You know I have a Christmas angel manifest, right?"

"Yes, though I don't really understand it."

"I can grant Christmas wishes . . . a lot of us can facilitate wishes, but around Christmas, I get stronger than most. So — if you should happen to have a wish?"

Nelis said, "Actually, my life is going well — it's been wonderful since I met Xav again, and I don't need to touch wood when I say it."

Flick said, "I should think not. Wood need not be involved when you're moving in the right direction with the right people."

"You make your own luck?"

"More or less. Wishes come in when you need a bit of help, though. You don't, but you can always wish for someone else — as a proxy. That's what our George did, you know. He wished for a lovely Christmas present for his dad, because he knew Chas was lonely, and somehow, that present turned out to be me. George is a good person, and he wanted his dad to be okay when he's off spending time with Sarah — his mum — and her family. He hated to think of Chas being lonely at Christmas."

"Oh . . ." Nelis thought about the implications. "If it's something the other person doesn't want, though . . ."

Flick patted her arm. "Trust me, a Christmas wish doesn't do that sort of thing. It will work out in the nicest way possible, even if it seems a bit odd at the time. It always does. George, bless him, got exactly what he intended, although, as he was quite little, he didn't understand the way his dad and I would execute the wish. I expect you can guess, being as it was Christmas Eve." She chuckled. "It involved some truly horrible pizza and a great deal of tinsel. Anyway, think about it while you shower."

Nelis went to join Xavier in the shower.

With her arms around him, and her soapy hands gently massaging his shoulders, she thought of those closest to her — her wonderful elf man, who would be her husband in a few more weeks, her loving, accepting mother, and her eccentric dad. They were all happy in their way already. Snow and Daisy loved one another, and their joyous reunions were all the better for not having to negotiate the huge difference in their preferred lifestyles on a daily basis. Daisy could handle an eco-cabin and hay box porridge for a couple of weeks. Snow could bear with television and frozen peas for the same period.

Then she thought of Lucy, who had helped her out of a pit of shame and self-loathing with grace and practicality. Lucy, too, had her life the way she wanted it. She blazed with joy when she thought of her halfling lover and their soon-to-be baby girl. Lucy's life was odd in any case. She spent half of every year on an offshore island living a nineteenth century life as a camp companion. By the fortune of fate, Ferris Island was about the only place in the human realm where Lucy's beloved, Paris, could join her for extended periods without feeling ill. His father was human, but he had thrown hard to his water maid mother.

But there was Dequan.

Nelis knew and liked Dequan, but they weren't close friends. He was the cousin of a friend. She supplied him with tomatoes and herbs for his cooking, and he had more than once sourced a rare book title for her to give to Daisy. They had never had an in-depth conversation outside these areas. He was a nice man who was related to her friend and who ran a useful service called *Qin-Find* — nothing more. And yet, his happiness would mean a lot to Lucy.

She thought of what Lucy had said that morning at their breakfast.

I wondered if he could see Tamzin again, maybe they'd get together . . . Or, maybe they'd have a coffee, and reminisce, and he'd realise she's just a nice girl, and he could find out why she never said goodbye or contacted him again.

And Nelis herself had said, "Closure."

So, what if she could get closure for Dequan, and thus for Lucy?

She switched her mind to enjoying a shower with her lover, stepping back to let the soapsuds rinse away.

Xavier could be a somewhat solemn person, but as she stood facing him in the generous shower stall, with the water streaming down their faces, she saw his smile as wide and delighted as a child's.

I'm doing that for him. He loves being with me, just as I love being with him. We've had a whole year and – glory be – we have so much more ahead! We can go off on the galleons and visit that magic island . . . and bring a souvenir home for Frances. Maybe we might have a baby together, a half-elf to love. Mum would be thrilled to be a granny and Snow would suggest some god-awful ancient-grains porridge as a first food.

She got up on her toes and leaned to kiss Xavier. He put his arms around her, and they hugged. No imperative, no straining cock, no urgency, just pure joy at being together.

"I love you, Xav."

"Nelis. My Nelis."

Dry and dressed in her frivolous pink party dress, Nelis went to thank Flick, whom she'd be seeing later at the party.

"Have you thought of what I said?" Flick asked.

"Yes. And I would like a wish, thank you. I've thought out the wording."

"Good. The wording is important, but the *intention* is even more so. Speak when you're ready." Flick made a gesture and the café quietened around them.

Nelis said, "I wish Dequan Qin and his Tamzin will meet up again soon, and have their happy ending, whatever form that may take for both of them."

She waited expectantly, and Flick shimmered before her. Suddenly, she was dressed in a flowing white gown, with a halo of light above her head.

She lifted her arms out, waist height, palms up.

Behold me!

A beatific expression came over her face.

She trembled like the hologram of a cheerful Victorian angel for a few seconds before the light faded, the angel vanished, and she was just Flick Dark again — lovely, kind, and adored by husband, stepson, and small daughter.

"Your Christmas wish is granted, and it was a good one," she said. She gave Nelis a hug and a sisterly kiss on the cheek. "See you at the party, Nel — and if you have time, you and Xavier could come to our place for supper after new year."

"We'd like that. By the way, Flick — remember when I asked you about your wedding dress?"

"I do. In fact, I'm wearing it tonight, because it's the anniversary of the day we met. Have you got yours yet?"

"No — but I'm going shopping with Mum as soon as she gets back from playing catch-ups with my dad. We decided we'll get vintage party dresses, the nicest ones we can find."

Flick looked pleased. "Xavier will like that, especially if you can find something pink. Even if the dress is another colour, I should think you could have a pink ribbon. He likes you in pink. Obviously, he likes you in anything, or in nothing, but I can tell he likes pink. It *does* suit you."

"Count on it! There will be pink. But the point is, Mum and I decided we'll ask guests to wear their favourite things."

"That's a splendid idea. Is Xav on board?"

"He thinks it's brilliant. It means he and his friends can avoid wearing suits. Xav *has* a suit, but he's much happier in britches and a tunic. He'll have some wedding embroidery on it, I expect."

Flick said, "You do know George is likely to wear a T-shirt of his own design, patterned with gingerbread. It's his new Thing."

"I hope he does. Your George is the best argument I know for having a boy about the place."

"Sarah and Chas did a glorious job when they made George, even if they didn't intend to make a baby."

Nelis nodded, but she thought Flick had played her part as well.

CHAPTER ELEVEN: THE PARTY

Nelis, Christmas Eve, 2020

Frances and Niall le Fay lived in a terrace house not far from the terrace that served the castle bridge gateway to *over there*.

Niall was an elf, but Frances was human, as far as Nelis knew.

Niall claimed she had left hand magic, which smoothed life just a little, and which pointed to a fay ancestor somewhere in her family tree. Since Frances le Fay nee Eckmann was a redhead, he said it was possibly leprechaun blood in his lively wife.

When Xavier and Nelis reached the terrace, the place was lit up with fairy lights. The door popped open, and Nelis stepped in, neatly avoiding the two cats, Cherry and Pie.

A piece of card with an arrow on it pointed upstairs, so the party must be happening in the upper level.

Nelis, with Xavier close behind, started up the steep stairs.

"Greet you, Evangeline," she said to the le Fays' small daughter, who was mounting the stairs one step at a time ahead of them.

"Pear!" Evangeline clasped Nelis' legs, so she scooped her up and carried her the rest of the way.

She had disliked being called Pear Tree at school, but she didn't mind when Evangeline did it. *Why* Evangeline did it, she had no idea. Surely a child of two wouldn't know Winter Nelis was a type of pear? Frances and Niall didn't call her that — she thought they didn't know her one-time nickname.

Laughter guided them to the attic, which the le Fays had modified to include a veranda that could be screened in with shutters when it was cold. The room was decorated with flowers and a retro Christmas tree, strung over with red and gold felt fruit. The tree looked far happier than any artificial tree its age had any right to look. Presumably, that was the Frances effect.

Frances, resplendent in what appeared to be a sheet fastened with a gold nappy pin and confined with a gold lame belt, embraced Nelis and Xavier, acquiring her daughter in the process. "You made it!"

Xavier untangled himself from his cousin's wife. "We brought courting cake and a whole lot of fruit from the *Pear Tree.*"

"Perfect. Dump it anywhere."

Xavier conjured in the provisions from Nelis' car.

"Why the sheet?" Nelis asked.

"Why not? It's a lovely sheet. It has fond memories of the night we met. Niall has one too." Frances gestured to her husband.

Niall indeed had a sheet, which draped becomingly, making him look like a Roman emperor with pointed ears.

"Don't take any notice of them. They're mad," a dark-haired woman called from across the room.

"Hi, Kendy," Nelis said. "That surely can't be your Nicholas . . ."

"I'm not lugging someone else's baby about," Kendra le Fay responded. She was Frances' cousin, and her husband, Piers, was another cousin of Niall's. It was Nicholas whose birth had short-circuited the Christmas Eve party the year before.

Nelis reminded herself to ask Kendra about the odd story Xavier had told her about a courtfolk man who had gone courting mounted on a kelpie mare, and who had spent some time with Flick and Chas in the cottage, but right then didn't seem the moment. Instead she said, "Xav's promised me a set of your husband's *Orders of the Fay* books for my birthday. When I get them, do you reckon he'll sign them?"

"No problem. Make sure Xav gets the new limited edition. It's gorgeous. Illustrations done by a sort of relative of Piers — Pen Inkersoll. That is, her husband's mum was a le Fay before she married . . . oh, I don't know. Nicky, stop that. Go and play with Vange." She deposited her son on his feet, and he scurried over to Evangeline.

"Greet you!"

A familiar voice had Nelis turning to see Flick Dark with her husband and children.

"George, be a love and — "

"On it, Flick." George took his sister from Flick's arms and led her over to the other toddlers. He sat down, and Joyful plonked into his lap. They started sticking felt shapes to a board.

Flick hugged everyone. She and Niall were cousins, but she wasn't related to Xavier.

Nelis relaxed. Any gathering that included Frances le Fay was inclined to be disconcerting, but Flick was always a calming influence.

Footsteps behind heralded two more guests, Eve Adeste and Raphael Angelus, bearing an enormous bowl of cherries.

"No babies held you up tonight," Kendra observed.

"Rasputin held us up," Raph said.

"Don't say you brought him . . ."

"Don't panic. He's in the courtyard with a whole poached cod and some boiled carrots."

Kendra blew out her cheeks with apparent relief. "In case you don't know, Rasputin is *the* biggest and evilest fay tom cat ever," she told Nelis. "He sneaked through the castle bridge gateway and took up residence with Raph."

"I'm not expecting any births, but if I get a call I'll have to dash," Eve said. She looked hard at Frances. "I'll be visiting you in a month or so to check on them."

"Oooh, cherries!" Frances pounced.

"Them?" Niall glanced at Eve.

Eve said, "Haven't you told him?"

Frances stuffed a handful of cherries into her mouth. "Eve—"

"Never mind. Are we all here?" Eve wanted to know.

"Eery."

"What?"

"She means *nearly*," Niall translated. "There's a girl Frances met down at the markets. She's coming and bringing a plus one."

Frances swallowed. "I think they just pulled up. Will someone go and bring them in? Jess hasn't been to the house before. Raph, you go. I need a word with Eve."

"*We* need a word with Eve," Niall said.

Nelis helped herself to the bowl of cherries. This was the first Christmas Eve party she'd made it to on the correct date, but she knew Frances' friends already, though she hadn't quite worked out who was related to whom, and how. They were all mad, anyway.

"You were saying about your husband's books," she said to Kendra, who was the only other purely human woman present, as well as being the sanest.

"Oh, yes—the illustrator being a connection. Usually that's a recipe for disaster, but Pen's been a pro for years. She's best known for *The Magic Cat,* but she's quite a big name—she exhibits. She has something in the Twenty-Twenty exhibition in Adelaide. It was meant to run for six months, but they've extended it. See it, if you have a chance."

"Is it just her stuff?" Nelis asked.

"No, twenty artists with one piece each. Jonathan Blarney, Marianna Mackenzie, Danya Quick, Dan Fanshaw, and someone I'd never heard of before who did an odd-shaped piece . . . ah, yes. Sass Delaney. Then there was a portraitist who did a self-portrait. She's just branched into illustrating, too—a new fantasy trilogy by Emily Jade. There are exhibitions of fabric art, too, and sculpture."

The door opened again to admit Raphael Angelus, shepherding a young woman in a green column dress wreathed with pink daisies that swept her toes and a young man in parchment-coloured britches and tunic.

Nelis felt her eyes trying to bug and she gasped.

Frances got in before her. "Jessie! How spectacularly gorgeous you look! Where did you get that dress? Is it vintage?"

The girl smiled. "No, I got it from a place in Lady Lane— *Fairings*. Do you know Otto Fairling?"

Frances shook her head.

"No, well, his mother owns the shop. She has some lovely stuff, and she does custom work. She did this for me—the flowers are centaury."

"That's so perfect!" Frances beamed at her. "Do you mind if I go shopping there?"

"Why would I mind? Jacaranda Fairling is happy for me to spread the word."

Frances switched her attention to Nelis. "Seems I might not be attending your wedding in a sheet after all, Nel. I fancy something very gorgeous with cherries on it."

Nelis nodded approval. Redheads didn't normally wear red, but cherries and Frances were the perfect match.

Jessie grinned at her. "Hi, Nel. Lovely to see you with—"

Don't say it—don't say with your clothes on . . .

Jessie didn't. "With Xavier."

"You know one another?" Frances broke in.

"Slightly. We met at the *Pear Tree*—that's a pub—last year.

I'm afraid I was responsible for her getting a drink of salvi-ation, which somewhat disagreed with her. I hope I'm for-given?"

"It was fine," Nelis said.

"Good. Nel, you remember Asher?"

Nelis managed a smile. "Yes, I think so." She held out her hand to the very young man who looked ready to sink through the floor. "I'm Nelis Winter, Asher. I've seen you be-fore, but I don't think we've ever met officially."

He took her hand. "Asher Castleby, mistress."

Jessie gave Nelis a reassuring nod. "Ash, I'll leave it to Frances to introduce you, since I don't know everyone either. This is our hostess, Frances le Fay."

Frances said, "Welcome to the mad house, Ash. It might be easier if we label everyone, but for now—I'm Frances, and Mister Elf Ears is Niall, my husband. Our daughter, Evange-line is the cutie in the party dress in the corner.

"Missus Dark-and-Cuddly is my cousin Kendy le Fay, and Tall, Fair and Handsome is her husband Piers, who is Niall's cousin. That's their Nicky pulling Vange's hair. It's his first birthday, so we can forgive him if Vange does.

"Let's see—Impossibly-Beautiful and Dark-and-Cheerful over there are Flick and Chas Dark with their big George and their little Joyful doing felt patterns.

"Serenity-Personified in the tunic is Eve Adeste, my mid-wife, and the Gorgeous-Greek is her man, Raph Angelus, who is slave to a terrible cat named Rasputin who fortunately isn't here tonight.

"Since you know Nelis, I assume you also know her fiancé, Xavier Partridge . . . and that's all of us.

"Everyone, this is Jessie Centaury and her friend Ash, whom I hadn't met until now. And that makes a dozen adults plus four kids. Four visible ones, anyhow."

She beamed around at them. "Welcome to the Christmas

Eve party chez le Fay. Now, do whatever you like, eat what you want—there are books, and drawing things and some musical instruments and a player—oh, we've got *the* most gorgeous album called *Magic Fiddle* from Arts in Tune. Put it on, Niall . . . I defy anyone not to dance. And Jess, please tell me exactly where I can find that shop, because I want to order my custom dress with cherries."

Nelis seized another handful of real cherries, and she offered the bowl to Ash Castleby.

She noticed he was looking anywhere but her.

"Ash—step outside with me for a minute," she murmured.

She went to the door and walked halfway down the stairs as fiddle music danced into being from the party room.

She sat on a step and patted the place beside her. "Sit down."

The boy sat.

"Look, Ash, when situations like this happen, we can either pretend they didn't, or we can embrace them. I know you saw me wearing not very much at the *Pear Tree*. I'm not an elf, but Xav is, so I know about the Hot. We both saw you there with Jessie, but we were rather caught up in what we were doing.

"Now, I don't know Jessie at all well, but I expect she had a nice time with you and asked you along to the party as her plus-one friend. You wouldn't be expecting to see Xav and me here, but it's *okay*."

She glanced at him and saw his cheeks were a dark red.

She cleared her throat. "So, this was your first Hot. You were very sensible to go to the *Pear Tree* and find someone lovely to teach you the ropes. Xav and I got together on *his* first one, and since neither of us had a clue what to do, it was a proper mess. Xav ended up in a quivering mess and I was sobbing in the ladies' room. We're fine now, obviously! I'm sure you're fine, too. Are you seeing Jessie again after tonight?"

He gave her a tentative smile. "She hasn't said anything about that, but I hope we could have tea together sometime. Or go dancing. She's lovely."

"I know she is. Maybe you can go out with her. Xav and I go dancing sometimes. Now, let's go back in and eat some of that party food, shall we? And we can dance."

He nodded. "Thank you, mistress."

She said, "Thank *you*, Ash, for talking with me. Do you know the shop Jessie was talking about?"

"Oh yes. Mum works there."

"Maybe I might go there — *my* mum and I want some gorgeous dresses for my wedding in February."

Ash Castleby got to his feet in the elastic fashion of a young elf man, and politely offered his hand to help Nelis up. She didn't need the help, but she reflected she must seem quite middle-aged to him.

She accepted his hand, and they returned to the party to find Frances canvassing names for her upcoming twins, while Niall loudly informed her that they'd think of something when the time came, but that the names were definitely not going to be Sheet and Cherry. He rather liked Seraphina and Gabriel or Barachiel or Francisco —

"Or Asphodel and Elodie," Frances said.

"Hebe," Kendra said.

"Ooh, I like that. Hebe and Nils, if one is a boy."

The party went on past eleven, by which time the younger children were asleep in a large bean bag, and George Dark and Asher had their heads together discussing George's idea that people should wear T-shirts with their favourite things to make it easier to know if they would be compatible as friends.

Asher was polling those present for things they would have on their signature shirts, and Jessie, who worked as a remedial therapist, was massaging Kendra's feet.

"You know what, Kendy's right. All these people are mad," Nelis said to Xavier.

He put his arms around her. "Merry Christmas, Nelis." He snapped his fingers and conjured a tiny parcel into her hand.

"No fair—mine for you is back at home."

"What would you have on *your* shirt, Nelis?" George asked.

"A pot of marmalade," she said.

"Excellent. It's easy to design and you could have some spilling out onto toast."

Nelis undid the tiny parcel to reveal a fine gold chain. From it swung tiny wooden ornaments—two pears, painted in bronze and green and gold so light that the grain of the wood showed through, a plump bird displaying finely barred wings, two wooden hearts, locked together, two gold rings, a ripe tomato, a pink party dress, an N and an X and the smallest jar she had ever seen.

"Oh, Xavier." She knew he'd made the charms. After all, he carved wooden ornaments and sculptures for a living, but she also knew that the smaller the pieces, the more difficult it was to show fine detail.

"One for every month of our magical year," he said.

Nelis wept. She had been right to use her Christmas wish for someone else.

She blinked and mopped her face with the handkerchief Xavier handed to her.

Frances tossed her a cherry as a clock struck twelve. "Merry Christmas, everyone, and Happy Anniversary to all of us," she said.

PART THREE: TAMZIN

CHAPTER TWELVE: LORELEI

Tamzin Campania, Delphinium Island and Sydney, December, 2020

For the second year in a row, Tamzin and Matin spent Christmas Eve at Delphinium House. Things were different this year. They had been living full time on the island for six months and had made considerable progress with the infrastructure.

Matin's music studio was up and running, and aside from the debut album, which they had called *Magic Fiddle*, they had produced three more recordings, working with indie bands Tamzin knew from the festival circuit.

Flexibility was the key to niche-marketing, so each production came with a separate agreement as to upfront payments, royalty sharing, or a blend of both.

The mixing desk which had caused Garret so much trouble at *Wildwood Studio* was part of the job lot of equipment Matin bought from Terry, but he'd also sourced a back-up, which could be used every time Mixmistress, as they dubbed the troublemaker, got up to her old tricks. Since Daylight was the accountant for *Arts in Tune*, she sometimes brought Garret, along with Shelley, Shelley's son Atapeke, and baby Daffodil to the island for the day where cherry pie, music, accountancy, and Mixmistress rehab took place in a welter of activity.

Shoe, Fou, and Hush were all delighted with the influx, which Tamzin thought was just as well, considering they'd be adding their daughter Music to the family in the new year.

The Hot was approaching fast.

Matin, who had been troubled about the effect of multiple beddings on Tamzin's six-month pregnancy, had finally given in to her order that if he said one more thing about it, she would spend Christmas with Gillan and Bran.

He looked so stricken that she quickly backed down, and recommended him to visit Doctor Lorelei, to whom she had gone twice for check-ups.

Lorelei, an elf maid in her late thirties, was seven months pregnant herself, expecting what she termed *an accidental son* to add to her two existing daughters, Gianetta and Bethlehem.

"She'll be going into the Hot more pregnant than I am," Tamzin pointed out to Matin.

"But you're human."

"I'm sure plenty of humans have elflets. Are you coming to talk to her, or not?"

To her considerable surprise, Matin agreed, accompanying her to Doctor Lorelei's clinic in north Sydney three days before Christmas Eve.

Tamzin had recognised her doctor's name when Branok St Ives first suggested her, but she had no reason to believe that Lorelei, who happened to be her old school counsellor's wife, would recognise a seventeen-year-old her husband had taught in Tamzin Campania. She didn't think they had ever met.

When it was time to be seen by the doctor, she got up and went into the office hand in hand with Matin.

Lorelei Herron smiled as she greeted them.

"Tamzin—and you're Matin, right? What can I do for you?"

Tamzin sat back in one of the chairs and Matin settled in the other.

The silence grew.

Doctor Lorelei consulted her notes and waited.

"What can I do for you two?" she asked again.

"I'm fine. Matin's the one with the problem," Tamzin said.

Doctor Lorelei's smooth brow creased.

Tamzin didn't blame her. Elves were almost never ill, and Matin, as usual, sparkled with health and vitality.

Tamzin said, "Matin, hurry up and ask her, or the appointment will be done before you get it out."

Matin bit his lip.

"Bleddy hell! I will, then!" Tamzin turned to the doctor. "Matin's worried about the Hot."

The doctor's eyebrows lifted, just a little.

"About me and the Hot, because of Music." She patted her rounded abdomen.

"Oh!" Lorelei said, "I would think the Hot will be fine. After all, you won't have to trouble yourself with holding. My husband is quite looking forward to it. He can go for broke and roar his head off in total abandon."

"But Tamzin is human," Matin said.

"Tamzin is in perfectly good health. Her blood pressure is fine, and she's gaining the right amount of weight. She's blooming in the way pregnant women are meant to, and so few actually do. I wish all my maternity patients were so well."

She looked from one to another. "If you're worrying about the effect on your baby, don't. You're well past the first trimester, and not so heavy as to make things uncomfortable or to launch a preemie. In my view, there's nothing better for a baby in utero than a healthy, loving relationship between the parents. Sex between committed partners tones up the muscles, enhances attachment, releases tension, and stirs up the feel-good hormones. I heartily recommend it."

She put her hand on her stomach. "I'm preparing for the Hot by getting plenty of sleep beforehand. Now—having said that, moderation is still the key. Try to restrain yourselves to no more than eight full scale acts over the twelve-hour period. That doesn't count hand and mouth action, if you enjoy that. Indeed, go for it! After all, next year you'll have a crawler . . . if not an early toddler . . . to contend with. The best way to manage that is to express milk, if you're still feeding, and let the little one go to your trusted carer, who should obviously not be an elf. I suggest you nominate someone very soon, so your baby can be used to being cared for by someone else. Tamzin's parents, perhaps."

"Not on your life!" Tamzin muttered.

"Oh? Is there something wrong with them?"

Tamzin considered Ada and Mister Sinister, or Paul and Adelie, as she sometimes thought of them these days, and she tried to formulate an answer.

Her brilliant, adaptable, chameleon, slippery, utterly amoral parents were un-formulate-able.

"I don't think you can call it wrong, precisely," she said, since Lorelei seemed to be waiting. "Let's put it this way — my childhood was so chaotic that I ran away when I was seventeen. I thought I was eighteen, but I wasn't. I've spoken properly with my father just once since then and with my mother . . ." She considered her few interactions with Breezy and the odd meeting with Adelie in *Fairings*, and continued, "a bit more."

"I take it they won't be part of your baby's life, then," Lorelei said.

"Most likely not. And if they are, it will be in our house, under our supervision, and possibly with both of them wearing electronic bracelets to give them a nasty zing if they try to leave the property with our baby."

"I see."

Tamzin added, "Matin's mum and dad already have grandchildren, so they'll be delighted to spend time with Music."

"They're elves, though."

"So not useful during the Hot. Not to worry, I have Bran and Gillan, my surrogate parents, and my foster brothers and their wives, and my friend Nell, who has grandchildren—not an elf among them."

Lorelei smiled, but there was a hint of trouble in her eyes. "Tamzin, I would never encourage you to have a relationship with folk you can't trust, but I do hope you have some close human friends or family. We can't be sure which way Music will throw, and it will be better for her if she sees that her mother isn't the only person in her circle who can't—well—"

Out of the corner of her eye, Tamzin saw Matin stiffen.

Before he could leap to her defence, she said mildly, "Doctor Lorelei, the day we met, Matin explained to me that elves aren't *better* than humans, but just different. If there's one thing I would like to see changed in my immediate circle it would be for my friend Bran—and his wife—to accept that he's almost half human and that there is absolutely nothing wrong with expressing that. They both believe Bran was lucky that Gill accepted him on that account, but *I* think she's equally lucky to have him. He works hard at keeping the pisky blood high—his words, and her thoughts—so she won't *go off and find a pointier eared prospect for her bed.* His words again. I think he was joking, and I don't believe for a moment that she would ever leave him, but they must both have the underlying belief that his human blood renders him somehow less. One of them even said one of his ancestors *lapsed* with a human halfling. They call her Ma-Ma, and they love her but . . ."

The doctor looked taken aback. "I didn't mean to imply that I think that way!"

"No, but you implied it anyway. My friend Daylight is a halfling but, unlike Branok, she accepts it, until or unless it affects her prospects." She didn't add that Daylight's halfling status was one thing that had stood in the way of her engaging with Gill and Branok's sons. "Do you have leprechaun friends?" she asked instead.

Lorelei shook her head. "My husband and I were born *over here.* I know a few colleens, but I wouldn't consider them as close friends." She held up her hand. "That's not because they are colleens, but just because they are patients, or acquaintances."

"Fair enough. You don't know any of the greenskins, then. The fullblood gossoons."

"Not well, no. The one I know best is Liam Dancey, who is married to Mama Tam, the midwife who attended me when our girls were born. I wouldn't say I *know* him especially, except in so far as he always looks pleased with himself on account of having Tam's attentions whenever he pleases."

"I don't know them, but with the colleens you know, do you consider them less than you because they don't conjure?"

"Of course not. I gather some of them could if they weren't indoctrinated to believe they can't."

Tamzin said, "The galleonfee can conjure, but they seldom do. I suppose, living in the confines of a galleon, there's not a lot of need to."

"Latent talent," Lorelei said.

"Maybe. My point is, that the gossoons and the galleonfee are a long way from human normal. Gossoons can't *pass,* and galleonfee almost never leave their ships. Nevertheless, they are just as fay as elves, and possibly more. I've never actually heard of a gossoon giving a human woman a baby, but I'm sure he could. They are loving husbands and fathers. Even a seaman probably could."

"She'd have to be extremely elastic," Lorelei muttered.

"To have the baby, or to accept that enormous todger?"

"Both. Although I know of a seaman wed to a rather odd courtfolk lady." She added, "I think I've got you all wrong,

Mistress Campania."

"No, I'm still the same Tamzin who came to you for help and advice. I trust you with my health and with Music's. So does Matin."

"I do," Matin said, nodding.

"It has also been pointed out to me that among humans, and fay, there are degrees of talent. I can't walk on a tightrope, although my father can. I can't conjure, although you and Matin can. I can't fix Mixmistress the mixing desk when it throws a tantrum, although our friend Garret can. However, I can play a leprechaun fiddle as well as any gossoon — or so I'm told. Can you?"

Lorelei's perplexed face smoothed out and she said quietly, "Point taken. I'm not musical. I see what you mean, and what's more, I see you're right. Just as I'm not less than my husband because he has a — what did you call it — a todger — and I haven't, and as he's not less than me because I can lactate and he can't, then humans and fay are not less than one another in any way." She inclined her head to Matin. "You were right to tell Tamzin that. I can see why she wed you."

Tamzin grinned at her. "Doctor Lorelei, I wed him because he smuggled a come-to-me into the heel of my shoe the day we met. Since that day, I have always been dancing on love. And this is despite our friends the godbrothers, who are as green as any gossoons I've ever met, informing us that only a man of the green way can craft a proper come-to-me. Mind, I knew that already since I learned how from the colleens of Balla Cloiche." She turned to Matin. "Did those poteen-brewing reprobates ever give you that come-to-me they threatened?"

"No, they accepted that your wedding ring had done its work."

Lorelei looked from one to the other in amusement. "I take it you two believe in these things?"

"We're living proof that they work," Tamzin said. "Besides, I have one here—" She tapped the shamrock pin Tiernan Flute had given her from his sister, Nuala. "This is to tell me when my friend Nuala Lightheart has come back to Balla Cloiche to visit her mammy and da—and I'm invited." She smiled at Matin. "I can thank my lovely husband for that intervention, too." She added, "By the way, you needn't worry about Music not knowing other humans. I belong to a group of women who call themselves Dames with Dogs and most of them are human—I think. My friend Nell is."

Lorelei said, dryly, "I know some of the Dames. They're formidable women who take charge of their health and well-being."

"As a group, there's almost nothing the Dames can't achieve," Tamzin said.

"Then I withdraw my concern. It was meant kindly."

"I know."

"But obviously, you couldn't let it stand as originally expressed."

"Exactly."

Lorelei smiled. "Then I think we can conclude this part of the discussion. Is that all, my dear?"

"Yes, thank you—" Tamzin paused, and she said with a rush, "I don't especially want to go into hospital to have Music if I can avoid it."

"I understand that. For some births, hospitals are the best and safest place, but for someone of your health profile, I think we can avoid it. Is Matin going to see to the delivery?"

"Matin's going to be with me, but I'd rather he was there as my husband and Music's dad rather than as a baby-catcher. When I was with the clan *over there*, babies were born at home . . . sometimes a tree maid would help. I understand water maids like your midwife will, too, but I don't know any."

"I think you might be well suited by another midwife I know—Eve Adeste. She's going to help me this time with our son. We've decided that since he's not going to be an easy child, we should have him eased into the world by someone calm and kind who can come to us at home. Mama Tam obviously can't come to us here.

"Eve's an elf maid who keeps company with a fay-touched human. If you like, I'll give you her man's number and you can arrange to meet." She conjured a notepad and scribbled a name and number, which she passed to Matin. She cleared her throat. "Just one thing—Eve's not qualified by human medical standards, but she comes highly recommended. One of her other clients is a human married to an elf, so you can ask her anything you like, knowing she has experience with your particular pairing."

She glanced at her screen. "Time's nearly up. Just pop up on the bed for me, Tamzin. I'll check on your baby's position."

Tamzin popped, as requested, and lay smiling as Lorelei's capable hands felt around her stomach and sides. "What are you going to call your baby?" she asked.

Lorelei said, "We haven't decided yet. Something suited to a child who is going to be a challenge."

Tamzin said, "Oh yes. My friend's dog is like that. His name is Cherry Pie von Atapeke."

"Atapeke," Lorelei said consideringly. "Atapeke Herron. It has a certain ring to it."

"Why do you think he's going to be a challenge?" Tamzin asked. She had no such feelings about Music. "You've mentioned that twice, now."

Lorelei paused, apparently deciding what to tell them. Finally, she said, "If I explain to you that he was conceived one night when I was in a shocking temper and the conception included a hot cloth and an iced one, although admittedly after the event, maybe you'll understand. Just take it that I was *not* in a good mood, and that I was *not* gentle with my man. I didn't harm him, but he may have felt a trifle shaken afterwards. I'm not suggesting parental mood at conception *necessarily* makes a difference, mind you."

Tamzin remembered her original bargain with Matin, that planting their child would involve roaring, commands and some resounding slaps.

She remembered the revised understanding and considered the actual event. It had been an unstoppable force, long and sweet and surprisingly calm.

As she considered that, she thought of the upcoming Hot. Gillan was taking charge of Fou, Shoe, and Hush, while Daylight's mother, Dell, was delighted to take care of her granddaughter, Daffodil, along with Daylight's dog Shelley. She had suggested she felt unable to deal with Atapeke, so Gillan St Ives was taking him as well. She'd told Tamzin, privately, that if it became necessary, her dog self, Lady Velvet, would manifest and sort out Atapeke with a paw on the neck and a sharp nip on the rump.

Tamzin was still contemplating their plans when Matin helped her down from the examination couch and they farewelled the doctor and left the clinic.

"Are you satisfied now?" she asked.

"Yes."

"Do you think we should contact the midwife?"

"I think that's up to you, my dolphin."

"I wonder if she does waterbirths," Tamzin mused. "We could go down the cliffs at home and launch Music into the sea near the Charm Line."

Matin said, "What about that seaman?"

"I don't think he'd be a problem. Meri's baby is due around the same time as Music. I expect she'll deliver underwater. Maybe you could ask her. She doesn't like me."

Matin laughed. "She thinks I'm a poor example of a man

with a todger incapable of its duty."
  "Music is proof that's not true."

Chapter Thirteen: The Hot

Tamzin Campania, Delphinium Island Christmas Eve, 2020

The Hot came in during the early hours of Christmas Eve. Tamzin had been half asleep, listening to the faint swish of waves, and conscious of Matin sleeping behind her, with one arm curved protectively over her baby bump.

She felt him stir and realised he was awake, and tense.

She reached back behind her and found his cock, hard and pulsing.

Here we go.

She jack-knifed, curling on her side, and manoeuvred him inside.

"Don't hold back."

"I can't." He sounded as if he might be gritting his teeth.

"That's good."

She snuggled against him.

"What about you?"

"I'll get mine sooner or later. Just you concentrate on —"

He groaned and stiffened as he shot.

Tamzin chuckled. "I was going to say, on enjoying the moment. Cloth, please."

A soft cloth materialised at her hip. She mopped up and rolled to face him, bringing his face to her breasts. "Relax a bit," she prompted.

He sighed, and she knew he was already stiffening again.

Well, he could wait a little while. Just as he enjoyed some discipline, she'd discovered he also enjoyed the pleasurable pain of full arousal and being made to wait.

She waited until she heard a hiss of discomfort before she got to her knees.

Matin rolled onto his back and held out his arms, but Tamzin shook her head at him in the faint light. "I'm going to have some fun." She let herself down and rubbed her cheek over his balls before settling to her favourite occupation.

Matin squirmed, and she gave him a smart tap on the leg. "We've spoken before about unseemly bobbing," she scolded.

She went back to her luxurious sucking.

"Tamzin!" he almost wailed.

"Oh, you go ahead. I'm perfectly happy here."

His hands came down, and she smacked them away.

"No. Remember, we decided you'd never have to try self-pleasuring again."

"But—" He tried to sit up.

"Stop that. Just lie still."

She continued to suck, running her tongue over to velvety skin. After a while, she added her hands, gently rubbing and pulling.

She remembered how excited the beau, her manifested courtfolk lover back on Summer Island, had got when she pleasured him, and she sat up abruptly.

"Conjure pillows behind you, so you can watch."

He squirmed again.

"Master Campania! Do as you're told! I have ice."

He must have managed to focus, because he was suddenly propped against pillows.

"Now, you watch my hands . . . watch them smoothing, and sliding and massaging, and when you can't stand it any longer, you can let go. But keep your hands where I can see them."

He smiled.

She smiled back. He trusted her.

Tamzin smoothed and rubbed and massaged. When she heard his breath beginning to catch and saw his eyes widen, she reached into a bag she had hung on the bedpost and unwrapped a soft package.

Matin said, "What are you—"

Tamzin pushed the package against his balls, and he screamed, caught his breath, arched high and shot, roaring with the effort.

She stayed with him, delighted with the effect.

"Great—bogle!" he gasped, when he finally flopped back, spent. "What did you do to me?"

Tamzin displayed the contents of the package. "It's a bag of frozen peas. Even better than ice, don't you think? Better coverage."

His eyes were still wide. "What are you going to do with those now?"

"Cook them for dinner. But first, I thought we'd test their efficacy as a retardant." She laid the package gently on *his* package. "Keep them there for half an hour or so and we'll get some sleep."

He nodded and held out his arms. Tamzin snuggled down against him, stroking his chest.

"Your hand is cold," he murmured.

"Mmm. Never mind."

She woke to find him dangling a bunch of grapes to her mouth.

"Yum!" She nipped off a mouthful and chewed happily. "Ready to go again?"

"Sorry."

"Don't be silly. Shall we go full wild dolphin on this one?"

"If you like."

"I like. I need a bit of resistance to get in the mood, though." He rolled onto his face.

Tamzin rubbed his bum and bent to nip it.

"Ouch!"

"Nonsense." She pressed his legs apart. He clamped them shut. She tried again. "Stop giggling, you."

"I'm not giggling. I'm—"

She gave him a smart push and he fell out of bed, onto a pile of pillows Tamzin had thoughtfully put there earlier.

She jumped down after him, sat on his cock and bounced.

Matin, laughing, slid lower in the pillows, and she flung herself forward to kiss him as they came together.

They were still laughing when they went to sleep.

The Hot dissipated around midday, and Tamzin, exhausted, nestled down in the bed. "I expect bread and honey and tea," she murmured.

"Yes."

"Then we can go for a walk up the cliffs and stir up Mariner and Meri."

"Is that a good idea?"

"Yes. I want to see him dealing with Meri. You did say she couldn't drown him?"

"She can't."

"Afterwards, we can have a tub and I'll cook dinner."

He hugged her. "I like that program, Mistress Campania."

"So do I. That's why I proposed it . . ." She slipped into sleep, to wake with the sun suggesting it was close to four o'clock, and Matin bearing a plate of bread and some tea.

"How do you think Olivier and Nessa managed at Fiddler's rest?" she asked, as she consumed bread and honey.

"I don't know. It's not our business."

"I know that, but I was thinking about Aunt Mim. Won't they disturb her?"

"I doubt it, but Aunt Mim might disturb them."

"What?"

Matin chuckled. "I've never heard Costas in full rut, but I'm assuming he can be loud."

"Costas—" Tamzin considered the grey-haired Costas Capricorn, who had played the lyre on *Over There,* her upcoming second album, which they intended to release on their wedding anniversary. He was at least seventy, short and compact with a strong nose, an aggressive beard, and a comfortable paunch. He had prominent brows over dark eyes which twinkled with what she saw as ferocious good humour. "You mean he and Aunt Mim are lovers?"

"What did you think they were?"

"Aunt Mim introduced him as her friend. I assumed he knew your Uncle Robert."

"Not at all. He's an old friend of the family—he knew Mim when she was a girl. She married Uncle Rob, as you know, directly after she was sponsored, and Costas soothed his sorrows with a mädchen who was older than him by a good bit. She went to glory about four years ago, and Costas came over to visit Mim." He sighed. "Pity he wasn't around when *he* showed up, but he was happily involved with his wife then."

"I see." *He* was Shades, aka Himself, aka Wayne "Duke" Ellington. Matin still hated to mention his name.

Matin kissed her mouth with slow enjoyment.

"Do you need to go again?"

"No . . ." He kissed her again. "Mmm, honey."

Then he said, "Costas chanced to come over two years ago today. Mim wasn't expecting him, and he'd forgotten about the Hot, if he'd ever known."

"Oh."

"I gather she was *very* pleased to see him. As you know, we can deal with the Hot alone, but it's not a nice experience. I believe Aunt Mim was sobbing in her room, gazing at a photo of Uncle Rob when Costas arrived . . ."

"And very soon she wasn't sobbing?"

"I assume not. She says she'd never been so well rogered in her life."

"Your Aunt Mim said that?"

"According to Costas she did. She was happy with Uncle Rob, but he was a good twenty years older than her . . . and . . ."

"And human," Tamzin supplied.

"I was going to say, he was a romantic person. If he'd been particularly —"

"Horny?"

"Yes. If he had, he would have probably been coupled up with someone long before he was forty."

Tamzin bit her lip, trying not to laugh. It seemed her beloved Fiddler's Rest had not seen a lot of rest since she left it on the morning of her wedding.

Something struck her. "Exactly what *is* Costas?"

"What do you think he is?"

"I assumed he was Greek."

"He is — but he's also a herdfee. His family are hereditary goat herders from Arcadia."

"That's an island in the Star Pin."

"Did you ever get there?"

"No — the only islands I spent much time on were Summer and Stella Orris. I also went to Dawn, and spent a few days on Bodhran, waiting for the fleet. I remember Foss Chancery, my pilot to Bodhran, mentioning Arrival, where there's a gate, and Bayeux went to Heather Island. Someone must have mentioned Arcadia . . . Bayeux, maybe." She frowned, remembering. "One of Foss Chancery's selves was a herdfolk man, I think. I sketched him while I was on Bodhran. Is that the same as herdfee?"

"Yes. You don't see too many of them *over here,* although I gather there are some in the Mediterranean."

Tamzin said, wonderingly, "Just when I thought I'd learned everything about you . . ."

"You never will, my heart, any more than I'll ever know

everything about you."

She said, "I'll tell you *anything* you want to know."

"I know . . . but I'm happy to have some surprises."

Tamzin pushed her hair back. "Last year, the Hot came on later . . . into Christmas Day."

"Yes."

"Does that mean it might come back?"

"Probably not. It's always unpredictable. Do you want to keep a bag of frozen peas just in case?"

"Do you? Did you enjoy that?"

"I hate to say it . . . but I did. There's something about being stirred up to the peak of readiness before having a bag of frozen peas smashed against one's balls. There's this endless second when things could go either way — shrivel like a tomato in the frost, of go off like a rocket. You ought to try it sometime."

"I did."

"I mean, on the receiving end." Let's see . . ." He tickled her left breast. "Maybe here, or maybe . . ." He reached down between her legs.

"It might startle Music."

"Not a chance. Remember, we have it on Doctor Lorelei's authority that sex is safe."

Tamzin got out of bed. "I think we'd better go for that walk. Dress me?"

"Don't want a tub first?"

"Not much point, if we're going to provoke the seaman."

Matin laughed. "My inventive love, you have a point."

He clicked his fingers, and Tamzin's green elf dress assembled itself around her.

She smoothed it over her bump. "Otto's mum said this wouldn't fit if I put on a lot of weight."

"Music isn't weight. She's a creative promise."

"No knickers?"

"No knickers."

"I'll let the sea wind cool my twat."

"Your—"

"That's what Bluebell called it, when she offered me knee knickers before I learned to ride."

"Your hob friend."

"Yes." She bent and rummaged through the clothes she'd discarded the night before.

"What are you after?"

"My come-to-me. Nuala was coming in summer, and it's summer now."

After she'd pinned it on, they set out from Delphinium House, past the sturdy little fruit trees they had planted the Christmas before, and on past the buildings already taking shape for next year's summer festival. They intended to hold a small introductory one in June, when Music would be three months old.

Tamzin followed Matin up the slope on the pink granite that led to the cliffs and waited while he opened the invisible gate.

They stepped forward into *over there.*

"Greet you, my fairyland!" Tamzin called cheerfully, waving to the bright sea and the jewelled islands that made up the Charm Line.

Her heart lifted, although she had been happy before.

"How shall we do this?" Matin asked.

They had recently found that having her wrap her legs around him was uncomfortable for them both.

Tamzin looked down at the shining granite. "We could have a mattress, or—if I bent over, and you put your arms around me, would that work?"

"You'd be leaning out over the cliff."

"I know. I trust you."

He nodded slowly.

"Untoggle me."

Tamzin did, laughing. "I thought the Hot was over?"

"It is."

She twanged him. "Well, here goes."

She raised her skirts to thigh level and flipped them up, leaning forward as well as she could.

Matin's warm, reassuring arms came around her, under her breasts. "Relax."

She let herself go loose, leaning out over the water.

"Ready?"

"Ready as ever!"

Matin pressed into her, warm against her skin, rocking himself deeper.

Tamzin kept her gaze on the waves breaking against the cliff, not so very far below. The seaman's rock and the path the fay goats used was out of sight, so it must be high tide.

She purred, feeling salt spray on her face.

"Oh, that's so *good*."

Matin, still bracing her with one arm, brought his second hand down to touch her.

"Ooh!"

Do I press back against him or forward into his fingers . . .

The flutters began, making the choice academic. His hand grew urgent, and she inhaled sharply, expelling the breath in a long, controlled sigh.

On the next breath, she panted, and her eyes blurred before everything erupted.

Her body jerked, and Matin hurriedly brought up his supporting hand, crying out in her ear as she wailed with pleasure.

She was still spaced out when she heard applause from below.

She opened her eyes quickly to see the seaman, Mariner van der Strand, seated on the submerged rock.

"Well played, master and mistress!" he called.

He brought both hands towards his upstanding cock . . . no, that really *was* a todger.

A green-silver hand rose from the depths like the lady of the lake and grasped the todger before he had a chance. It pulled.

Mariner van der Strand yelled and vanished under the waves, only to re-emerge lying on his back, with his wife, naked but for a belt of shells around her hips, sitting astride him, facing his feet and bucking furiously. Her svelte shape was bowed out with her pregnancy, but she continued her motion hard and fast until the seaman opened his mouth to roar and they vanished in a maelstrom of bubbles.

Tamzin choked, and Matin gently pulled her back to the vertical.

"Did you enjoy the show?" he asked.

"I did, actually. I often wondered why Shay and Cornelius enjoyed watching . . . although Cornelius pretended he didn't."

"Pretended?"

"He always disapproved, but he could have gone away. Kate said Roland enjoys watching her with Claudette, so maybe it isn't all that uncommon. Why was she facing his feet?"

"I assume that was to get friction against those impressive balls."

"Yes, that would work—oh, look!"

There was movement below, and the seafolk surfaced. Mariner had one arm under his wife's legs, and the other around her shoulders. He grinned up at Tamzin and Matin, ducked his head and kissed Meri passionately on the mouth.

"She'll bite him," Tamzin said.

But Meri didn't. She tucked her head against her husband's shoulder and sighed.

After a bit, she looked up at Tamzin. Her mother-of-pearl

eyes were calm.

"Greet you, Mistress Campania!" she called.

"And you, Mistress van der Strand."

"Call me Meri." She patted her husband's shoulder. "This one seems determined that we are to be friends."

"I'd like that. What will you call your baby?"

"Kelp. I used some to bind this one's todger to his leg until he agreed to be mine."

"A fine name," Matin said.

"We think so. One day soon, you will come to us on Seadown Island. We'll take you to our sea cave. *No harm.*" She smiled at Matin, showing sharp teeth. "Never fear I'll bind *you*, elf man."

"I don't fear you, but *she* just attacked me with frozen peas."

Meri's eyes widened and she looked puzzled.

Tamzin said, "I'll bring some for you to see."

"To *use*," Meri said with evident relish.

"I think we'll bid you a fare-thee-well," Mariner said. Still holding Meri, he jack-knifed in the water and vanished.

Tamzin said, "Did we just make friends with them?"

"I'm not sure. My dolphin, you do get into some mad situations."

"I know. We'd better go back and get that tub."

"Yes, but first—" Matin removed a small package from his pocket.

Tamzin took it. She had his Christmas gift with her as well . . . the second volume of court portraits detailing their love story.

"What's this?" she asked, examining the silky bag.

"Open it, but be careful."

She opened it and she peered inside to find tiny packets done up in galleonfee cloth.

"These are dyeflower seeds from the tor, and some others

that come from the Star Pin," he said.

Tamzin said, "However did you get them?"

"Your Shay asked his wife to harvest the dyeflowers, and your friend Caddy Hildebrand had a relative of hers—Davey Inkersoll—send word to the fair wind fleet. His sister, Mistress Sorenson, collected seeds on Stella Orris, and from some of the other islands. Then, I went to see Roland, and Kate gave me some of the broderie rose seeds. Evidently, they come true to their parents. Then of course there's bedding thyme and chamomile from Skyside. Misty got that for me. They're all marked up with their names."

"That is so perfect, but—will they grow *over there?*"

"I took advice on that from Mistress Ondine, via Bran St Ives. She said they normally won't, but since Delphinium Island is in a league of its own, and fay-touched, there's a fair chance at least some of them will flourish. After all, seadown grows up on Ferris Island."

"I don't think I know that place."

"It's an island out in the ocean the V-S company uses. Evidently, there's a gateway there, which probably explains the seadown. With that in mind, we can bring some soil from Skyside to get them started."

"My little piece of *over here*," she said.

"Yes . . . the same as you had at Fiddler's Rest, but much more."

Tamzin hugged him. It wasn't only the seeds that Matin had sourced, but the implied greetings from friends she sometimes missed.

"There are notes from some of them, but I didn't bring those to the cliff, in case the wind caught them."

"You already know what I have for you—but here it is."

Matin received the small book and leafed through it. "This one has more pages," he observed.

"That's because we've been living together for six months,

so I've found more and more reasons to love you."

He kissed the little book and chuckled. "Once, I asked you what you loved about me, and you said, my balls."

"I do!"

"Then is there a painting of those?"

"Not yet, but in next year's book there may be one of a bag of frozen peas. How you did roar! I thought you'd never stop spurting."

"It's most undignified," he said.

"Ah, but remember, *I* like to watch. Seeing you going off like that makes me excited."

He smiled at her, slowly shaking his head. "And you look so ethereal and so beautiful in your green dress. Who'd have believed you were so —"

"Misty calls me a hoyden," she said.

"If what you mentioned about Misty, Lars, and the turnips is true, Mistress Mistley Haydale should not call the kettle black."

They returned through the gates and back down to Delphinium House, stopping along to way to choose the best place for Tamzin's new garden.

"I'll call it the Painting Garden," she said, hugging herself.

"That will be good, and you can render your colours right here."

CHAPTER FOURTEEN: FAMILY

Tamzin Campania, Sydney and Skyside December, 2020

On Christmas afternoon, Tamzin and Matin drove to Sydney to fetch Fou, Shoe, and Hush from Gillan and Branok, who had been minding them.

"Merry Christmas, darling," Gillan said to Tamzin, while Bran shook hands with Matin.

"Good news," Bran added.

"Oh?"

Gillan's face lit up with more joy than Tamzin had ever seen her express. "Zen and Githa are expecting!"

"That's wonderful," Tamzin said.

"Don't try working out the months since they were married," Gillan said.

"All right—I won't." Tamzin hugged her friend. "How's Mull?"

"Pouting," Branok said.

"I am not," Mull St Ives said, emerging from the kitchen. "You're blooming, sister of my heart." He called over his shoulder, "Morgana, can you bring that dreadful little dog out here?"

"Coming." Morgana, Mull's wife, looked very much like her cousin Daylight as she came out, holding a shrilly snarling small dog in both hands.

Gill took charge of him. "Atapeke, do you need another nip?"

The snarl changed to a silly grin and a wave of a plumed

tail.

Tamzin picked up Shoe in one arm and Fou in the other. "Fou, can't you keep your son in order?"

"He doesn't try," Gillan said. "Can someone call Daylight and find out if Garret's gone off the boil? I want this fiend out of the house."

"They'll come as soon as they can get out of bed," Mull said tolerantly. "So, Ma spilled Zen's news."

Gillan looked sheepish. "I wanted Tamzin to know."

"You'd better spill our news too," Mull said.

"You're expecting?" Tamzin asked.

"Are we? Morgana?"

His wife said tartly, "That's for me to know and for you to discover."

"Oh."

"What news, Mull?" Tamzin asked.

"We're expanding *Lanner's* — talent nights. We're hoping to offer a recording contract to the winning act to make it worth-while." He turned his bright blue gaze on Matin. "Is that something *Arts in Tune* would sponsor? We'd pay your usual fee."

"I should say so."

"Come and we'll . . ." Their voices faded as they departed.

Morgana took hold of Shoe and put her spare arm through Tamzin's. Although she looked a lot like Daylight, she smelled of summer gardens rather than coffee. "Come and sit down, Tam. No need to rush off."

Gillan and Bran soon joined them, and Branok said, "I wasn't talking about Zen and Githa when I said we had good news. I meant Ondine Delphinium has responded to the first report I sent her on your lease of Delphinium Island. She's pleased with the progress, and she has no qualms."

"That's good," Tamzin said. She had still not met their landlady, but she hoped her ship betrothal was going well.

That reminded her of the letters she had from *over there*. She hadn't read them yet.

She said, "Is there anything else we need to do?"

"No, just continue as you are. There's no real need to make reports to me. I can come and see you now and again to observe."

"That's not the way it usually works."

"No, but you're the daughter of my heart, and Master Campania is your heart's companion."

His words caught at the heart in question, and she felt impending tears.

"What's wrong?" he asked.

"Nothing. I just compared the way you and Gill are with the way my parents are."

She thought of Breezy and Clem, the disassociated temporary Dames, and of the self-congratulatory Paul and Adelie.

Morgana said, "You're making your own family now."

"So we are," Tamzin said.

The kettle squealed, and Branok grimaced and headed back for the kitchen. "Gill, where did you . . ." His voice blended with the whistle.

Gillan sighed and went to sort him out.

Morgana leaned over and whispered to Tamzin, "So are Mull and I making our family. We're not announcing it yet because we decided Githa and Zen should bask a little longer in the sunshine. Their baby will be born first, but we both wanted *you* to know."

On Boxing Day, the Campania family gathered for a traditional lunch at Bellflower Cottage. This year, the gathering included Lirrin and Bay, Misty, Lars and their children Dickon and Florence, Matin and Tamzin, Olivier and Nessa, and Aunt Mim and Costas.

Tamzin glanced at Costas and wondered how she had ever

taken him for human. He so clearly wasn't. He caught her eye and winked. "Survived the Hot for the second year in a row," he remarked. "How did the rest of you weather it? Not worn out in the nethers?" He turned to Lars, Tamzin, and Nessa in turn.

They mumbled unconvincingly.

Misty tossed her head and remarked, "There is no need to be vulgar, Master Capricorn," just as if she hadn't confided scandalous details to Tamzin in the pantry twenty minutes before.

She handed baby Florence to Tamzin. "So you can get into practice . . ."

Six godbrothers turned up with their father and grandfather, and they and Olivier vanished into the cellar.

Tamzin, cuddling Florence in one arm and Shoe in the other, pondered that she had never seen Eamon the Red's wife, or his mother, come to that. No doubt they existed and no doubt they were cherished. She decided to ask Lirrin and Misty to introduce her.

Lirrin bounced Dickon on her knees and Fou retired under the table with his disreputable stuffed bear.

Loud song burst out from the cellar and Nessa sprang up in a jingle of silver.

"That's it! I'm going down."

"Dear me," Aunt Mim said as the girl vanished down the trapdoor. "Whatever are girls coming to these days?"

"Says the woman who rode me into next week shrieking *tally-ho—up and at 'em. Aghhhhh!* at the top of her voice," Costas said, not quite in a whisper.

Lars slapped his knee and gave a great gust of laughter.

"Aye, that's a reet good one, Mim!"

"Hush now, Master Capricorn, and you, Master Haydale, or I'll be forced to cut the connection," Misty proclaimed.

Matin and Bay got up rather suddenly for a stroll outside.

Tamzin thought they were probably off to have a good laugh.

Two godbrothers climbed speedily out of the cellar carrying a huge amphora of something potent.

"Blessed Christmas be wid ye," they gabbled as they fled.

"And the rest of you can just go too!" Nessa sang out from below.

Tamzin rocked Misty's baby and her own sleepy pup and smiled.

"What is it, Tamzin?" Lirrin asked softly.

"I was just thinking—*bleddy hell* I love this family. By the way, might I meet Master Eamon's lovie sometime?"

Lirrin said, "That's a lovely notion, darling. I often go to take tay with the colleens in the family, but they don't come here on account of the cellar."

"What's wrong with the cellar?" Tamzin asked.

"They won't say, except that the old bottles down there keen at them. Maggie did say something about bottled bansidhe, but I have no notion what she means."

Tamzin didn't know, either, but the tiny mystery delighted her.

"We might go to the New Year ceilidh, and you can meet them there," Lirrin added.

CHAPTER FIFTEEN: FATE OF A ROSE

Tamzin Campania, Delphinium Island, December, 2020

It was two days after Christmas before Tamzin took the time to open the letters that had come with her new seeds.

She had planted these already, trusting to the magic of Delphinium Island and her earnest desire for them to flourish.

She sat on the veranda, with Fou sleeping beside her. Shoe and Hush were playing a complicated game with one of the fay goats that had taken up residence on the island. Tamzin called her Nanny Lutana because she was moon pale with golden eyes.

Matin was in the kitchen, ostensibly making tea, but she thought he was probably giving her privacy to read her letters.

Music stirred, moving rhythmically under her ribs, and Tamzin patted her daughter absently.

She opened the first envelope, which was made from seadown paper, presumably traded from Dawn Island.

The letter from Andorie Sorenson, lady of *Unicorn*, began conventionally enough, wishing her well and hoping her music and sketches continued to delight her.

The next lines informed her that Arne Halfdan, her young galleonfee lover, had met his bride on Stella Orris, *liked what he perceived, and sealed the bargain with a bedding. All is well.*

Tamzin smiled, remembering Arne. She hoped Viviana was all he desired and all he deserved.

One curious thing, Andorie added in her neat, looped script.

Arne is now with the golden fleet, but he spoke with me and his family before he embarked to Lobo Dorada. *He and Viviana spent a night on the island, as I said, consolidating their pledge, and down in a cave where they took shelter, they found a rose charm on a ribbon.*

Tamzin blinked, and reread the sentence, before she continued.

Arne said it is the one that belongs to you, his Mistress Rose. He says he is certain, because he had the opportunity to examine it closely while you were tutoring him in his manners.

Well, that was one way to put it . . .

He left it there in the cave, with the idea that you might return to look for it. I thought it unlikely, since your husband, who wrote to me via my brother, is not, I think, the man who gave you the rose. Nevertheless, if you would like to have your charm back, you may send a message to me again, via my brother. Davey is my twin, and so he can discover me wherever I sail, and conjure to me. When the blue lady blows us back to the iris of the sea, maybe I could find the charm for you and one day you can have it again. Until then, Stella Orris will keep it safe.

Whatever you decide, dear Thomasine, (although your man refers to you as Tamzin) we of the fair wind fleet will always think of you kindly as one of our own.

Tamzin slowly folded the paper. Suddenly, she was back on the deck of *Unicorn,* sailing with Nuala, making friends with Andorie and helping Arne with his hands-on experience.

She sighed. It all seemed a long time ago.

It *was* a long time ago. She felt she had lived several lifetimes since then.

The next note was written on heavy cream embossed paper. Tamzin opened it and found it was from Kate Maple, or Kate Banister as she was now.

This one was short, and stated that she, Roland, and Claudette would be glad to see Tamzin and Matin at the next

Midwinter ball, regretting that they hadn't come to the last one, although, as she understood, they were newlywed at the time. She was, affectionately, Mistress Kate Banister. She added a postscript to say that she had recently visited her maman, who was still displeased with her, and that Master Treelove had expressed a wish that darlin' Thomasine might come to play the fiddle with him again.

A second postscript added that Kate's darling little sister, Briar, was very well and happy, and so was her brother, Cornelius. Her dear sister Honorée was, as always, delighting in sunshine and her husband and a welter of children.

Tamzin reflected that this would seem most odd to most people, but she understood the beautiful complications of the clan. Kate was a semi-sister to Briar and Honorée through their father, Zeph Maple. She was a semi-sister to Cornelius through their mother, Juliette Myriad. Shay Beech, the son of Darragh Treelove and Dia Beech, was unrelated to any of them. Therefore, it was good and well for Shay to marry Honorée, and for Cornelius to be with Briar. All the same — it was a good thing, surely, that Kate had *married out* of the clan, choosing Roland Banister who, on Tamzin's brief acquaintance of him, seemed to be a tolerant and attentive husband for bubbly Kate. His old friend Claudette also attended to Kate, and Roland enjoyed watching, so it was a good thing all around.

A third postscript stated that Kate rather thought she was expecting, and did Thomasine think it was a good idea to mention this to Maman before it became visibly evident?

It might end her displeasure with me, but if it does, then I may feel slighted as if I were nothing but a vessel — this was heavily underlined — *for her grandchild, but should I say nothing, Maman may feel slighted and be more displeased . . .*

Perhaps you might wish to draw Maman being displeased? It would amuse Roland no end.

Tamzin put this missive aside and sat considering it,

wondering whether Kate was being funny intentionally. Probably so.

Maybe we can visit Kate and Roland – and Claudie – before Music comes. And we shall *go to the ball if someone remembers to send an invitation! I'll see Gill about the dressmaker to remodel my gown . . . or maybe Jacaranda Fairling might do it. Or I might have Jacaranda make me a gown in purple taffeta, and a white one too.*

She smiled at the thought. At one time, she had wanted to wear green, but all manner of colours pleased her now. She thought of Otto's wives who liked to wear blue, and Dahlia, who favoured glowing yellow, and who had married Garret in a sunshine-coloured gown. Gillan generally wore strong jewel tones. And then there was Nell, who treasured a wrap-around skirt in strident orange.

I'll start a new series of blog posts for The Elves Made Me Do It *. . . all about colour and clothing.*

The third and final letter was written in charcoal pencil on paper made from pounded leaves. In it, Shay and Honorée sent one of Shay's inventive blessings, much love to the sister of their heart, and news of a new baby, a colleen they named Verity. Shay thought they might stop now, but who knew when the whim might take Honorée to quicken again? If so, he would receive the babby with a glad heart and open arms. They hoped the dyeflowers would grow well in the strange world *over there,* and reiterated that Shay's da, Darragh, hoped to play again soon with darlin' Thomasine. He wished to see if the fiddle kept its tune.

These notes, and the promise of meeting Nuala Lightheart again as soon as the come-to-me gave her a sign, made Tamzin feel not so far away from her old friends as she had supposed.

Who'd have thought I could have penfriends in Fairyland!

She put aside Shay's letter, smiling, as she always did when she thought of him. She decided she would introduce him to Music soon after she was born. He would hold her baby and pronounce a long and beautiful blessing.

The smile lingered as she recalled Olivier's Nessa routing the godbrothers, and Aunt Mim's unlikely activity during the Hot. *Tally-ho ... really? And no doubt Master Capricorn was cheering her on.*

She called to Matin, and over tea and courting cake, she pushed the letters across for him to read.

"What will you do about your rose on a ribbon?" Matin asked when he had finished his perusal.

There was nothing but friendly interest in his face, but at the back of her mind Tamzin recalled his once-expressed regret that she had bought her green elf dress to delight another man. She had corrected him on that point, but the rose was another matter entirely. That linked her to her first love as the dress couldn't.

"I don't know," she said honestly. Then she amended it to, "Yes, I do! I'll try the visualisation trick Nell taught me before we went to Adelaide for the Twenty-Twenty Exhibition back in February."

"Do I know about that? The trick, I mean — not the exhibition."

"Probably not." She told him about Nell's *what to do about the husband exercise.*

"Obviously, you decided I was more of a help than a hindrance," he said.

"You will never be a hindrance. The visualisation showed me that right away. Only this time, it's about what to do about Dequan's Elf Maid rose."

She closed her eyes, and as Nell had suggested, she pictured herself reclaiming her lost treasure.

She pictured it as it had looked when Dequan gave it to her, as a perfect tea rose in miniature, faintly scented and dewy-fresh to the touch. Where had he got it? Had he bought a single flower, or a potted bush — and was she right in thinking the rose pots outside his Gilchrist flat might contain Elf Maid roses?

Of course, he hadn't lived there when he was seventeen, but he might have taken them along when he moved to the flat in — well, sometime after December two thousand and nine but before September two thousand and seventeen was the closest she could get to knowing that.

She tried, and failed, to remember exactly what he'd said when he presented it. Something to do with a catalogue name, and the parents being Fairy of the Forest and Darling Thomasine. And he'd had to search to find the nearest he could get to a green rose.

She pictured it as it had been when she immersed it in clear resin during her first few days at Macquarie Bay.

She'd hidden it from her parents but taken it with her when she ran away.

She'd worn it for years because it was a tangible link with Dequan and with her Tamzin identity.

She remembered how bereft she'd felt when she realised, once landed on Bodhran Island, that she'd left her rose behind. She had no idea how it had happened, as she rarely removed it. Maybe the ribbon had finally frayed or snapped.

In any case, she'd lost it, and after a while, she'd begun wearing the orris stone disc in its place.

She shook herself. This wasn't helping. She had to visualise getting it back, not tracing its provenance.

She pictured someone handing it to her, or conjuring it to her, possibly wrapped in galleonfee cloth.

Don't be silly. What would you do with it? Pin it to a curtain? You have a dolphin to wear now.

She remembered her curious hesitation to contact Dequan upon her return from Dancing Tor. Branok had offered to let her call him right there from the office.

She'd refused, telling Branok she didn't have his number.

She could have called his parents, or failing that, she could have gone to visit them.

She'd justified her refusal by saying she wanted to go to him unencumbered.

True, she had finally gone to the address Branok had found for her, but on seeing him with his girlfriend, she'd left without attracting his attention.

What was it Daylight had said?

Fight the bitch for him!

And she'd said . . .

Why would he be with a bitch?

Afterwards, Daylight had come out with something that amounted to, *If you'd really wanted him, you'd have made a move. He's probably turned into the symbol of everything you never got to have . . .*

Daylight was right. Dequan, over the seven years of exile, *had* become a symbol. So it was with Dequan's rose.

She opened her eyes.

Matin was looking aside, with his gaze grazing past her cheek as it used to do when they first became lovers.

He doesn't want to see my face.

"Matin, look at me."

He looked. "Have you decided?"

"There's nothing to decide. Andorie's right. I don't want, or need, that rose now. It belonged to the person I was then, or to the person I was trying to hold on to. I'm not that person now."

"No," he said.

"If I'd still wanted that rose, do you think I'd have said *forever* with you?"

"No," he said.

"So, I don't want it, or need it. It can stay on Stella Orris."

He smiled. "I'm the one with the love story books."

"Yes, you are. You're the only person I would ever have made them for. Although maybe I'll make something like them for Music."

"*We* shall make one for Music."

138

"Oh?"

"I don't draw, but I can write some words."

PART FOUR: NELIS

CHAPTER SIXTEEN: FROCKING UP

Nelis, Sydney, New Year's Eve, 2020

Daisy Comice returned from her reunion with Snowland Winter early on the morning of New Year's Eve.

If she was disappointed that Snow preferred to go on an expedition to Patagonia rather than celebrate New Year with the woman who had loved him for over three decades, she certainly didn't say so to their daughter.

Instead, she got out of the taxi—Snow would have had a conniption if he'd known about that—and knocked on the door of the flat Nelis shared with Xavier during the week.

Ordinarily, Nelis and Xavier would have gone to their place *over there* for the holiday, but Nelis was expecting Daisy.

They hugged on the doorstep.

Nelis noted that Daisy looked a bit drawn.

"Bad flight?" she asked, switching on the kettle.

Daisy smiled. "Not half so bad as it would have been if your dad had his way. He'd worked out a wonderful way of saving money. The fact that it would have sent me bouncing around the country with ten-hour layovers was nothing."

"I'll bet."

Xavier, hearing voices, wandered into the kitchen. Nelis was pleased to see he'd put some pants on, but less pleased to note they were drawstring pixie britches.

She thought Daisy knew Xavier was an elf, but she wasn't sure. She didn't remember telling her.

Not that it matters what he wears . . . Mum spent years with

Dad in his eco-recycle pants.

He hadn't got a shirt on, but Daisy wouldn't disapprove. He came up to her, rumpled from sleep, and held out his arms.

"Greet you, Daisy. Glad to see you back. How's Snow?"

Daisy went into his arms and gave him a hug. "Nice to see you, too, Xav. Snow's fine. Probably ankle deep in guano by now. Or do I mean iguanas?"

"I expect so," Xavier said. "I'll get the coffee, Nel, and some toast and fruit. You talk to your mum."

Nelis ushered Daisy out to her small back garden, where she grew herbs and tomatoes. "Let's sit out here."

Daisy said, "The thing is, *he* would take those flights without a thought. He'd either sleep on the airport floor between the seats and get fallen over by women with hoovers, or charm someone into letting him into the exclusive lounge."

Nelis perceived they were still talking about Snow.

"I know he would."

"So it's not that he—"

"Mum, I *know*. I lived with him for years, remember? Snow is Snow. He'll never change."

"No," Daisy said.

"Mum, do you ever wish you hadn't met him?"

"God no!" Daisy ruffled up her greying hair and smiled. "If I'd never met Snow, I'd never have had you, and besides, he's fun."

"He is, when he's not being infuriating."

"He puts the surprise into life. He says he's coming to your wedding."

"I won't hold my breath."

"No, he'll come if I have to put a halter on him and drag him."

"As long as *you* come . . . let's get that coffee and hit the shops. We're going to a boutique called *Fairings*. I hope you don't mind, but we're meeting someone first. She's going to take us there."

"Why? Anything wrong with your car?"

"No, but the place is a bit hard to find."

"Oh, one of those. Back in the eighties, Snow and I were wandering about in London—or was it Glasgow? Anyhow, we walked into a shop that sold the best baps you ever had."

"What the hell is a bap?"

"Maybe I mean a bath bun. Or a Sally Lunn. Anyway, the next day we decided to go back and get some more. You can guess what happened."

"You couldn't find the shop."

"Right. We walked the streets for the whole week we were there, and pretty soon everywhere started looking familiar. We ate baps every day, but they were never *the* baps. At least, I don't think so. By the time you've eaten twenty-seven baps, it's difficult to be sure."

"Jessie knows where this shop is, and she says she'll take us straight there."

"Retro party frocks?" Daisy asked.

"Better than that. Custom made."

Daisy's eyes sparkled. "Can't wait. Is Xav coming?"

"No, he's not allowed to see my wedding dress before the day."

"Just us and Jessie, then. Jessie who?"

"I expect so. And her name's Jessie Centaury. I met her at a party on Christmas Eve."

"Your dad and I spent Christmas Eve on a tropical island."

"Really? Which one?"

"I don't know. Someone Snow met took us there in an odd little sailing boat. There were lots of islands, actually."

"Bap Island?" Nelis suggested, and Daisy laughed.

Nelis perceived a new family catchphrase had been born.

They went to meet Jessie, and it turned out the party included Asher Castleby as well.

Nelis hadn't expected him, as she'd supposed Jessie had merely invited him as a plus one to Frances and Niall's party.

She greeted him with a friendly smile and introduced her mother.

"Ash, this is my mum, Daisy Comice. Mum, this is Ash. His mum works at the shop we're going to."

Daisy said, "Hello, Ash. Glad to meet you."

She didn't question Ash's inclusion in the party. Daisy Comice had long ago learned to roll with the surprises.

They left Nelis' car in a car park and caught a train to Circular Quay.

They walked to the Rocks and thence into a tangle of small streets and lanes dating from colonial times.

"Keep an eye out for Lady Lane," Jessie said. She was wearing jeans and a skimpy top with unnecessary sunglasses, and she seemed altogether less unusual than she had at the *Pear Tree* or at Frances' party.

They walked past the lane twice, and Daisy said she supposed they mightn't have baps today after all.

"Are you hungry, Mistress Comice?" Asher asked.

Daisy said, "No thanks, love. I had breakfast with Nelis and Xav."

Nelis interpreted the reference to the others, and just as she finished speaking, Jessie stopped.

"There it is!"

"Couldn't see it for looking," Daisy said.

Jessie said, quite seriously, "The best things in life are often like that, right, Ash?"

Ash nodded.

The bells over the door tinkled a gentle tune that Nelis remembered from the fiddle album they'd listened to at *chez* le Fay.

"You found us, then," the woman behind the counter said. She was embroidering cherries on the fine white lawn of a bodice.

Frances was here!

"Greet you, Mistress Fairling," Jessie said.

"Hello to you, again. I see you've met Ash."

"Yes, he came to the party with me. These two ladies want party dresses." Jessie indicated Nelis and Daisy.

"I think we can accommodate that," the woman said. She wore a long gown of graduated purple and purple drops in her ears next to her swept up greying hair. She focused on Nelis and Daisy. "What did you have in mind?"

Daisy said, "Nelis is getting married in February. She wants something striking and I want something that doesn't shriek *mother of the bride.*"

"I should think not!" Mistress Fairling laughed. She looked at Daisy. "Would you be happy in something long and rather ethereal, with meadow flowers? Or would you rather have a snazzy number in a strong colour with a fifties silhouette?"

"The second one," Daisy said.

"We can make you net petticoats, but I suggest you go through the fabric samples I have in that bin. Look along the rails to the right, too. The dresses are all different, and you might find something already made up that takes your eye."

Daisy moved purposefully over to the rails. She began taking down garments and holding them against herself.

Asher went to her and offered to hold the possibilities.

"And for you?" Ms Fairling asked Nelis. "I don't do traditional wedding gowns, but if you go through to the workroom, you'll see a board showing some of the special orders I've done." She indicated a curtained doorway, and Nelis went through.

A dark-haired woman sat there at a table laid with tea things. She was placidly embroidering on a large piece of undyed fabric.

"Hello, I'm just looking at the pictures here," Nelis said softly. The woman looked up with soft hazel eyes.

Elf eyes.

Her ears, not quite so pointed as Xavier's, were half screened by her wavy locks.

She looked a little vague, and Nelis wondered if there was something wrong with her.

She said, "Hello, sweeting. Do you have little ones?"

"Not yet," Nelis said, a bit taken aback.

"I love the little ones. I have a son, you know, but he's man grown. Maybe one day soon he'll find a maid and make babies."

"Is your son called Asher?" Nelis asked.

"Yes! He's a Hot child, and so am I." She smiled. "It's odd how many of us there are. Mind, I found a loving man that year, so I did far better than my mother. Mind, she found better luck the next time."

"I'm glad."

Nelis, unnerved, stepped past to look at the selection of photographs on the board. She realised some of them were paintings, beautifully rendered in soft colours.

"These are so good!" she said.

The woman got up and glided over to look. She pointed at one of the paintings. "This is Zandie. I hadn't seen her in a long while, but she came to us for her wedding dress. She let me look after her little dog, Fou, while Jacaranda worked with her. I love the little ones. She brought him back to see me again, and I helped put up her hair when her mother gave her earrings."

Nelis gazed at the picture. It was a full-length portrait of a woman standing at a mirror, which reflected the gown so she could see both sides at once. It was breathtaking, showing a slim green sheath covered with a magical overlay of rainbow colours. The woman wore a sparkling bracelet and an unusual pendant.

Nelis leaned closer, and saw it was a wooden dolphin. She touched her wrist, where Xavier's wooden charm bracelet lit up her life every day.

The dolphin wasn't his work. It was unpainted, and not quite as professionally carved, but it was beautiful.

It shouldn't have gone with the bracelet and the gold hoops in the woman's ears, but it did.

Memory tweaked, and she recalled Xavier telling her about a wedding in the Fairy Gardens, where the bride wore rainbows.

"Was this woman married about six months ago?" she asked.

The elf woman said, "Yes. I went to watch. She didn't see me, but that didn't matter. My Zandie is happy. Fou was there, too."

"Is Zandie your daughter?" Nelis hazarded, although the woman didn't look old enough.

"I used to look after her when she was a wee thing. She called me Nanny Lu."

"Is Lu your name?"

"Lucida. It means light. My mother named me that way because she loved me anyway."

"It's a pretty name. I'm Nelis. That's a kind of pear."

The woman nodded.

"Zandie is a pretty name. It suits her."

"Yes, her big name was Alexandra, but she is Zandie to me. She wed an elf man, which is good. Zandie always said she was an elf."

"Is she?"

"No, she's human, but to see her dance with the children to Darragh's fiddle, you'd have thought she was one of them."

She indicated another pair of dresses on the board. They were both blue. "Jacaranda made these for her daughters-by-love when they wed her son."

Nelis realised she was talking about Otto and his wives.

"Those are beautiful, too." She added, "Lucida, what colour would look good on me, do you think?"

The elf looked her over, smiling. "Have you noticed the gown Jacaranda wears?"

"Yes."

"Then something like that, but in dark pink and green layers. You'd look like a camellia."

Nelis wasn't sure if *camellia* was the way brides should look, but the idea caught at her imagination. She knew Xavier loved to see her in pink.

"Thank you," she said. She put out her hands and took Lucida's. "May I look at your embroidery?"

Lucida nodded assent towards the frame.

Nelis went to look and caught her breath. The piece wasn't finished, but it showed a colourful scene she recognised as being *over there*. Children danced in a circle, as if playing ring a ring o' roses. Most of them wore small tunics. She'd seen elf children wearing those when she went with Xavier to their weekend home. One tiny child was dressed in a tunic with embroidery, and pink gel sandals. She was laughing.

In the middle of the ring a young leprechaun man played a fiddle made of wood polished to a deep shine. His mouth was open in a gleeful grin, and he seemed to be watching the little girl in the sandals.

Purple and white flowers grew about their feet, and in the distance ponies grazed. A willow tree drooped over a small pond, and sitting against it was a young elf woman, making an embroidery as she watched the dancers.

"This is gorgeous," Nelis said. "Do you exhibit? Someone I know said there's an exhibition of fabric art in Adelaide."

Lucida shook her head. "I just make embroideries of things I remember. I started this one when I saw Zandie again."

"Thank you for showing me, and thanks for the idea for my dress. I like it."

Nelis went back through the drapes to find Asher draped with garments over both arms, Jessie examining lengths of lace, and Daisy — not there.

"Where's Mum?"

Daisy called, "In here, love. Can you hook me up?"

"Changing room," Jacaranda Fairling said.

Nelis let herself in through double doors to the surprisingly spacious room where Daisy stood in front of a mirror.

"Wow!"

Daisy said, "Isn't it? Can you do up the hook?"

Nelis fastened the tiny hook and eye and stood back.

Daisy twirled. The skirt must have been over a hoop or net petticoats, because it stood out, before tumbling gracefully to Daisy's neat calves.

"Mum, you look *stunning.*"

"You don't think it's too much?"

"No, it's perfect."

The dress had a shaped neckline and three-quarter sleeves on a tight bodice finished with a belt. The colour was dull gold, but the fabric was printed with faint white stars in drifts and constellations.

"You look like a fairy-tale princess." Nelis lifted Daisy's long hair and twirled it into a bun. "We'll need to get you gold shoes, and I'm sure Xavier would make you a necklace."

Daisy said, "I have a necklace. Snow gave it to me before he went off to Paraguay."

"Wasn't it Patagonia?"

"Maybe. It's a tiny gold nugget he picked up on his travels and had set in gold."

"Is it hung on a yak's hair cord?" Nelis asked suspiciously.

"Yes, of course, but I have a gold chain my godmother gave me. I always meant to wear it for my wedding, but now I'll wear it for yours." She tossed her head and twirled again.

"Come and show the others," Nelis said. She opened the

doors and led Daisy out into the shop.

Jacaranda Fairling looked her over. "All right Asher, you can put those back, my dear. We have a winner."

Jessie said, "That's perfect, Daisy. I'll help you out of it."

They disappeared into the fitting room.

"What do you think?" Jacaranda asked.

"Mum? She looks lovely. I thought she'd go for something really bright, but that is classy."

"I agree that style doesn't need a lot of embellishment. Have you any ideas for yourself?"

"I looked at the photos and paintings, but nothing is really *me*. Then your assistant — is that what she is?"

"Yes, Luce is an assistant and a friend. She's wonderfully talented . . . All the lace you see in the shop is hers. She's a partner in all but name — and that's her choice. She prefers the workroom to front of house."

Nelis said, "She came up with an idea of dark pink and green layers. Would that work?"

"It might. Or maybe — how would you feel about a dress in one colour and an overskirt in the other? The front panel would be visible with the skirts looped back in paniers."

"Like Little Bo Peep?"

"Well, not quite! You could have a bit of coloured embroidery at the neck to bring the two together."

"That sounds good. I'll be wearing this charm bracelet." She held up Xavier's gift for inspection.

"We can pick up the little pear with the green shade, and the pink with the party frock charm. Are you having an attendant?"

"Yes, Mum. And possibly my friend Lucy, but that depends on when her baby decides to make an entrance. She has her own dress, which is green with flowers. She wore it to a court ball, and it has a high waist."

"Excellent. The two dresses for you and your mother will

contrast beautifully. What's your man wearing?"

"A fancier version of britches and tunic, I think. He might have wedding embroidery. He has a suit, but he doesn't seem very keen to wear it."

Jacaranda laughed. "At least in a tunic he won't need a preposterous stiff handkerchief in his pocket. Anyone else in the wedding party?"

"I expect Xavier will get one of his cousins to stand up with him, but the only other person is my dad, and if he comes at all, he'll probably arrive in a spaniel hair suit, or an eco-woven bamboo loincloth, or a penguin costume made from recycled feathers. Don't laugh. It's all too likely."

"I like him already," Jacaranda said. "I can have your dress ready for fitting in a couple of weeks. Your mother can take hers today."

"How much?" Nelis asked belatedly.

Jacaranda jotted down some figures. "You can pay over six months if you like," she said.

Nelis looked at the prices. They were high enough, but lower than she would have paid for a traditional silk and tulle number. "We can manage that," she said. "It's worth it, to be beautiful."

She nodded to the cherry embroidery draped over the counter. "I think the dress you're making there is for one of our guests. Frances le Fay."

Jacaranda flung up her hands. "How did you guess? She came tearing in here in pursuit of a little girl—my, how fast that child can run. Luce took charge of her, fortunately, and Frances said she wanted cherries for a wedding where everyone was wearing their favourite thing because, and I quote, she'd decided a sheet wouldn't cut it."

"That's Frances," Nelis said, grinning.

PART FIVE: TAMZIN

CHAPTER SEVENTEEN: GEENIE

Tamzin, Delphinium Island and Balla Cloiche, New Year's Day, 2021

It was Tamzin's birthday again. Actually, it was Alexandra Spenser's birthday, which was an odd thought.

Even odder was the arrival, by special delivery in a car with a dark blue V-S logo, of a small brown paper parcel. It bore no address.

"Who's this from?" Tamzin asked the driver, a tall young woman with fair hair that swept down her back and out of sight.

The woman shrugged as she unfolded herself from the vehicle to reveal high laced boots worn over tight jeans. She looked vaguely familiar, but Tamzin couldn't work out where she'd seen her before. "Don't ask me. I just do the deliveries. I came up here yesterday with a mad couple after an even madder young alpenfee man with *two* wives—twins, if you please—hijacked my ticket. Geese! I ask you! They kissed *all* the way and I think I heard her yodel! I debouched them somewhere near Milson's Point and now I'm here. The life of a V-S driver! I can't tell you my name, because a small but deadly hob man said I'm not to—my stars! Takk, I said to myself, Takk Engel, you are *not* to divulge your name to Missus Campania." She paused. "Bleddy hell! I just did!" Her eyes rounded with comical dismay.

Tamzin cut through the flood of talk. "Never mind all that. *Who* sent this parcel? Are you sure it's for me?"

"I guess so. The woman said it was for her daughter who was preggers. That's you, right?"

"Maybe."

"This woman ... Adeline Burns ... she said —" She clapped a hand over her mouth. "I think I'd better go before I do something else I shouldn't."

She widened her eyes again. "Sign here, eh?"

Tamzin signed.

An imperative yip made her look up, expecting to see Shoe doing something she shouldn't. Her pup was not in sight, but a narrow terrier face appeared suddenly at the window of the car. An odd lightning-bolt blaze divided the dog's face.

Tamzin stared. *I've seen that dog before . . .*

She opened her mouth to say so but changed her mind. "What's your dog's name?" she asked instead.

"Puffin." The young woman slid back into the vehicle, executed a three-point turn and drove off.

Wait — how did she get to the house? Isn't the gate up on the causeway? How did she know my name? I didn't have Fou then . . . let along Shoe.

Tamzin shrugged, perplexed.

"Who was that?" Matin asked from behind her.

"She said her name was Takk Engel. I think. What's that — Finnish?"

"Or maybe fijordfee," Matin said.

"That would figure. Her little dog is called Puffin. She delivered this." She proffered the parcel. "I think it's from Ada. Adeline Burns . . ."

"Are you going to open it?"

Good question.

"Can you de-hex it or delouse it or whatever?"

Matin took the package and laid two fingers on the seam. "It feels all right to me."

"I'll risk it, then."

They took the parcel inside, fending off Hush, who seemed

to think it ought to contain carrots.

Tamzin laid it on the table and untied the string that secured it. Then she unwrapped the paper to reveal an inner
layer of blue tissue paper.

The scent of lavender came to her, and she frowned as bits
of dried flowerheads fell free.

She unfolded the rest of the paper, reminded suddenly of
undoing the double wrapping that had contained her wedding ring.

The last fold fell away, and she stared at a child's tunic in
dull green. It was beautifully made, with flowers embroidered around the neck and hem. She looked up at Matin.
"This is what children wear *over there*."

"Some, anyway," he said. He picked up the tunic. "This
one is a festival dress—ceilidh dress."

She nodded. "Do you think it's for Music?"

"I expect so."

"But why would Ada—"

"Didn't you say she used the name Adeline Burns? That's
the name you told her she had to use if she was ever to have
any contact with her grandchildren."

"Yes, but how does she even know?"

"It's not exactly a secret, dear heart."

"No." Tamzin reached out for the tunic and shook it out.

"There's a note," Matin said.

"What? Where?"

He flattened out the wrapping paper. "In pencil, light . . .
almost as if it's just the pressure."

"More mind-games!"

"Shall I read it?"

"Yes, do."

"*Dear Tamzin—I have carried this about for long enough. It
never fitted any of our room sets because we didn't buy it. On the
other hand, it is yours, and I didn't quite like to dispose of it. Nanny
Lu, of whom I have few fond memories, and of whom you probably*

have none from that time, made this for you after I complained about her constantly bringing you home sandy and muddy from your walks. For some reason, this garment doesn't soil easily.

"I understand you are expecting our grandchild. You might like this for him, or her. It isn't a gift. I'm just returning something that is yours. Do whatever you like with it. Someday I may send you the kaleidoscope Angie had. By the way, do you ever paint peace lilies?

Adeline Burns."

Tamzin said, "Words fail me." She remembered the kaleidoscope. A tiny dancing lady had given it to her — or was that a dream?

Matin said, "I think this is an olive branch."

"I don't see why. I said they were welcome to contact me. There's no return address though — right?"

"Nothing that I can see."

"I suppose I *could* try the *DonandMilly* email address, although I don't know the extension . . ." She shivered. "I hope they're not going to keep stalking us."

Matin said, "It was a kind thought. You might have worn this when you went dancing with the children to the leprechaun's fiddle."

"Geenie," Tamzin said thoughtfully. "I think I might go to Fairings and see if Lucida will tell me who he was. It doesn't seem likely she'll say much, though. He who shall not be named seems to have that effect on folk. Lucida, Aunt Mim — even you."

"I'll come with you and see if I can help."

"Elf to elf? No, you have work to do."

Matin shook his head at her. "Tamzin, it's New Year's Day! And your original birthday. Let's go somewhere to celebrate."

"Yes, but —" Tamzin clapped her hand to her chest. "What on earth — oh!"

Matin smiled. "I think your come-to-me just sent you a sign. Your friend Nuala must be back in Balla Cloiche."

"Can we go there?"

"Of course we can! Want to bring the tribe?"

Tamzin considered two dogs, one disreputable stuffed bear and one lippy pony. "No. We won't be gone long. They can mind the fort."

"Better bring your fiddle." He conjured it for her.

The drive to the castle bridge gate took a while, but once through the gate into *over there,* they were soon at Balla Cloiche.

The village was deserted.

Tamzin frowned. "Where is everyone?"

"Didn't you say they go to the cliffs to signal the ships?"

"So they do. If we go to the pier, we'll see the fleet standing off." She felt a catch of excitement.

My fairyland!

Holding hands, they *went* to the pier, where many of the villagers were having an impromptu ceilidh while they waited for the longboats to come in.

"Greet ye, darlin' Thomasine!"

Tamzin turned to look down into the smiling eyes of Tiernan Flute.

"So, the come-to-me brought ye," he said.

"Sure, it did."

He indicated a petite colleen standing on the pier. Unlike the women of Balla Cloiche, she had brown hair. She was young and shapely. "There is me lovie, Aine Harper," he said with pride. "Is she not winsome?"

"She is, that." Tamzin found the leprechaun dialect coming back to her tongue. "Is she waiting for someone?"

"Sure, her mam and da are sailin' in wid me sister Nuala," he said. "Pastor Goodbook will be sayin' the words for us. Ye'll play the wedding tune?"

"I will! When will it be?"

"Soon as they set foot," he said.

Tamzin glanced at Matin, who was smiling. "You knew!"

"Maybe," he said.

Tamzin switched her gaze to the fleet, standing out to sea. She sought the butter yellow and white sail of *Unicorn,* but it wasn't there. Nor were the pink and sky blue of *Mermaid* and *Chimera.* The sails she saw were instead a uniform white, with large, coloured emblems on the canvas. She identified a gold wolf, and a purple butterfly, but the others were too far out to tell.

"What fleet is this?" she asked.

Aine, Tiernan's beloved, turned and said, "Golden fleet, mistress. Mam and Da sailed on *Lobo Dorada.*"

"Oh!"

Tiernan beckoned to her. "Come to meet darlin' Thomasine an' her man, lovie. Friend o' Nuala."

The meeting filled the time until a longboat pulled in, coming alongside the pier. The leprechauns streamed out to help the passengers to alight, and Tamzin went with them, longing to see Nuala again.

There was her friend, rosy and bonnie, perched in the lap of a gossoon who must be her husband. She held a baby in her arms. Two small girls stood at her knees.

Aine stretched out her hands to the older couple who had to be her parents.

Nuala rose, steadying herself on her husband's shoulder and handing him the baby.

She stepped up onto the pier and turned to take the child back from her man. He had one little colleen clinging to his hand.

"Let me, master," a cheerful voice said, and one of the dark-haired oarsmen lifted the third child and swung her up out of the boat. "If you please, mistress?"

Tamzin stretched out her arms to receive the small girl. Then she turned to the oarsman. "Greet you, Arne."

He started, swaying, and for a moment she thought he might fall overboard. He recovered himself, looking up at her in astonished recognition. "Mistress Rose! Thomasine Forest!"

"Actually, my name's Tamzin Campania now," she said. Someone took the child from her, and she reached out both hands.

Arne clasped them.

"So, you found your love," she said.

He smiled. "I did—and thanks to you she has an accomplished man for her bed." He glanced at her baby bump. "And you found your man of the rose?"

"Well—not the one I was expecting, but yes—I have a forever love." She looked up at Matin, who was patiently holding the child. "This is my husband, Matin Campania."

"And you are Arne Halfdan," Matin said.

"I am, and the luckiest man in the world, since I'm wed to a dark-haired beauty and have a brown-haired one as a friend."

"Elegantly put, man," Matin said rather dryly.

The passengers had disembarked, and the longboat was drifting away from the pier. Arne took his place and drew on his oar. He shot one last laughing glance at Tamzin, called, "Be happy, Mistress Rose!" and the longboat was away.

"Darlin' Thomasine!" Nuala gave her a smacking kiss. "Here's our Thomasine, our Rose, and our babby Una—nearest we could get to *Unicorn* after the ship that sailed me to love."

The rest of the day tripped along happily. Donal Goodbook, the pastor who had blessed Thomasine and her fiddle years before, married Tiernan to his Aine, and much holy water and poteen was splashed about. Tamzin played the wedding dance for the couple, accompanied by one of Tiernan's brothers on the flute. There was a general feast afterwards, singing in the New Year, the wedding, reunions and a toast to Thomasine and her man and babby-to-be.

"I keep trying to tell them I'm *Tamzin*," she said to Matin as they took their leave.

"I think you'll always be Thomasine to your friends here," he said.

"I suppose so — I seem to have committed myself to coming back for another round of portraits. How am I going to have time?"

"Darling dolphin, I think you'll make time. These are good people, and they wish you well."

"I know. Aren't you going to say anything about Arne?"

"Why? What is there to say? He has good memories of you, and you of him. He has a brown-haired beauty as a friend. I think that's clear enough."

"He didn't mention finding the rose."

"There wasn't much time," he pointed out.

Tamzin watched the celebration fires sparking up and felt suddenly tired. "I think we'd better go home, Matin. The tribe is waiting for carrots, belly rubs, and lap time."

He put his arm around her. "It probably is time to go."

A voice behind them said, "Not quite yet, if ye please, darlin' Thomasine."

She turned in Matin's embrace and squinted into the dusk. A leprechaun man stood a little way off. It wasn't Tiernan or Pastor Goodbook, or Nuala's man Dublin Connemara, but his stance was familiar.

"Greet you," she said uncertainly.

"Sure, don't ye recognise me, lovie?"

Matin said, "My wife is tired, master."

"Not too tired to give a hug to an old friend? An older friend than ye know —"

Tamzin moved forward, seeing the fiddle slung to his back. "Master Treelove!" she said, wonderingly.

He smiled.

"I have a hug for you—of course I do! Matin, this is Shay's dad, Darragh Treelove."

"I know," he said. "If you remember, I saw your Shay some time ago, and his father, here, helped me to find out about Nuala for you."

"That's right." She put her arms around Darragh. "I'm so happy to see you again. It's been what—three years?"

"More," he said. "No blame to ye, dearie, but I'm glad I heard ye play the wedding song again."

She smiled. "I played it for my own wedding, too!"

"There's a marvel—how did ye manage that?"

Tamzin considered trying to explain a recording to a man who had never heard one and never would. Then she remembered with shame that the clan weren't simple.

"There's a way of making a copy of the sound, so we can play it any time we like. Something like a photograph of music." She knew he had seen photographs, because Juliette Myriad had some of herself as a young woman when she was being sponsored.

Darragh said, "Ah, Juliette has told me about that. Records, she called them."

"We use what came after records, with the sound stored in tiny pieces of metal. And do you know, I can even record *Follow Me,* by playing both parts and putting them together."

"There's a wonder," he said. "I wonder would ye play wid me—now."

"If you like. What shall we play?"

"*Grá Damhsa,*" he said.

"Yes! I love that!" She unslung her fiddle and passed the bow over the strings.

Darragh played the phrase again before they burst into the joyous tumble of music, playing the dance of love. Darragh started to dance, and Tamzin's feet remembered the cadence. They circled and played, their bows flying, until the final thrill of sound.

Tamzin's head spun, and she was glad when Matin put a supporting arm around her.

He said, "It was a privilege to hear you two playing together."

"Master Treelove taught me to play, and made my fiddle," Tamzin said. "I owe him my music."

"Thank ye, girleen." Darragh strapped on his fiddle. "I'm glad to hear your fiddle is in tune."

"Why wouldn't it be?"

"No reason. I'm glad to have had the chance to play with ye again."

"I loved it too. Maybe we can play again sometime soon. I know I haven't been to see you, but Juliette is displeased with me."

"Mistress Juliette has no reason to be displeased with ye, or with Kate. Indeed, I think in her heart, she's not. It just can be a habit hard to break and harder to admit an end to."

Tamzin reflected that she knew about habits and ideas kept past their use-by date.

She ventured, "Did you want to see me for a reason? Or did you come to Balla Cloiche for the wedding?"

"I did that, but mainly to see ye. I have something to say that ye might not want to hear."

She said hastily, "Is Dia all right? Shay and Honoreé and all your other darlings?"

"Very well, all. Eighteen grandbabbies we're blessed wid. Do ye recall how easily the fiddle music came to ye?"

"Yes. I love music, my fiddle is magical, and you're a wonderful teacher. The fiddle I learned on was an old hand at teaching, too."

"Oh, but I played that old fiddle for ye long ago, way back when a girleen I knew brought ye to listen. I'd play for the elf children, her little semi-sisters, and for you, who thought yerself an elf. I played and ye'd dance, and one day ye wished ye could play like me." He shrugged. "That wish hit me, an' I let it carry me. Just a little thing. But that little thing bound ye tighter to the music an' ye didn't want to leave . . . and it hurt ye. I've niver forgiven meself for that, an' Lucida niver forgave me either.

"Dia said it was not my fault, and music is a good thing to give, but—givin' a wish to a babby—" He turned out his hands. "That should niver have happened."

Tamzin leaned into Matin's embrace. It was his habit to be silent when challenges came, and his habit to hold her in his love while she worked out her response. Her mind spun, trying to process lost memories, fragments of which had come back through Aureate Shale, through Zen St Ives, through the strange Lucida and through her parents and even Shades, and now through Master Treelove . . .

She opened her mouth to say something, to assure him it didn't matter, that everything has turned out well, but only one word came out, in a whisper. "*Geenie*?"

Darragh nodded. "I was your Geenie, darlin', but after you were hurt, and taken away, and Lucida came cryin' and rantin' at me for givin' a wish to a babby, then I made meself a promise I'd stick wid me family up at the tor. I niver played for a human again, until ye came to us and loved me son for a time."

"I still do love him," Tamzin said. "I always will. He and Honoreé know that, and so does Matin. I love all of you at the tor—even Juliette." She fought down the desire to question him, and to scold, and she said gently, "*No harm*, dear Master Treelove. Zandie—I—was a cranky little thing. I brought the hurt on myself. I never wanted to wait for things I loved . . . until I was seventeen, and after that I waited way too long. Have you talked to Lucida lately?"

He shook his head. "Not in many years. She turned her face

away from me and I was sorry."

"She works in a shop *over there,* and she helped when I was choosing a wedding dress."

"Is she well?"

Tamzin hesitated. She didn't think Lucida was well, exactly, but she doubted if that was any blame to Master Treelove. That was probably down to her father, who had used her the way he used, or tried to use, everyone he pleased. For all she knew, he was still at it. And maybe Lucida's strangeness was partly down to genetics or — *bleddy hell!* She shivered with distaste. What was it Paul — no, *Mister Sinister* — had said so casually?

That's when we found out we'd hired a blooming fairy — Wayne's daughter. We didn't even know he had one. He'd knocked up some elf woman one Christmas. Lu was the result.

Did her father even know what his words implied? Wayne Ellington wasn't an elf — or not much of one — so if he'd got a baby on an elf maid during the Hot, it might not have been with her full and informed consent.

I ought to talk to Jacaranda Fairling. But what on earth could I say?

She was suddenly very, very tired.

Matin said, "We'll go home now, Master Treelove. I think Tamzin will want to come and see you all at the tor quite soon. Is that so, my dolphin?"

She nodded. "Yes. I really do. I have some more portraits to do for your collection, and I'd like to see Master Maple again, too. I heard from Kate, by the way."

To her relief, Darragh's face lit into a smile. "Dear Kate has found her path, although it's not what her mam may have wanted."

"I'll bring our baby to meet you all, too, when she's born," Tamzin said.

Darragh's smile widened. "We'll set up a ceilidh, an' maybe Kate and her man will come."

And Claudie.

Tamzin didn't say that, but she was sure the clan wouldn't mind . . . except possibly for Juliette. Indeed, Master Maple, Kate's blood father, would be pleased. He had once told his daughter she was a lucky one to be able to love twice over.

"Road rise to ye—Tamzin." Darragh turned and stepped into somewhere else.

Matin guided Tamzin back quickly to the castle bridge gate, and she slept all the way back to the island in the car.

Blinking, she realized they were home, with three vociferous animals demanding food and company. She smiled as she made the rounds with hugs, pats, belly rubs, carrots, and chicken and rice.

The last mystery of her life seemed to have dissolved.

Emily was coming through the gates tomorrow from the Harvest Hob with Sheelagh Applebee, who would hand her on to one of the Cornfellows to bring her to the castle bridge gate and hand her into Mistress Joan's keeping.

Her mother had made a gesture, she had a baby to prepare for, a festival to enjoy, and a husband to love forever.

She was content.

PART SIX: NELIS

Chapter Eighteen: A February Wedding

Nelis, Sydney, February 14th, 2021

Nelis Comice Winter married Xavier Partridge on Saint Valentine's Day.

They chose the Fairy Gardens as the venue because the payment for the statues of Jacobi and Barbara le Fay had paid for the wedding and led to new commissions.

Nelis' wedding gown was even more beautiful than she had envisaged, and Daisy glowed in her gold and white party dress. Snowland Winter turned up in a suit and top hat that looked as if he'd found it in an antique shop.

"Good God," Daisy said in wonder when she saw him.

"Used to belong to Great-Grandad Winter. It's been laid up in lavender for forty years. Thought I'd let the moths out." He grinned at her and handed her a ring with another chunk of gold nugget.

"From the digestive system of a Patagonian beetle?" Daisy asked, wiggling it into place.

Snow said, "Want to get married, Dais?"

"Sure, as long as we don't have to live fulltime in the eco-cabin."

He patted her shoulder. "We can go on as we are, but maybe meet up more often. We'll have the piece of paper, but we've always had something, right?"

"Baps," Daisy said.

Snow said, "We'll go bap-hunting for our honeymoon and

167

eat our way around Glasgow."

"I thought that was London."

"Glasgow —"

Nelis, attended by two parents who seemed to be starring in two separate Broadway musicals, and an extremely rotund bridesmaid in platform shoes, had never been happier.

The guests also looked like stars from their own private fantasies, wearing catsuits, wreaths of flowers, a dress seemingly made from book covers, velvet flares, and T-shirts depicting everything from a stack of gingerbread to a vintage racing car. Frances did not wear her threatened sheet, but a cherry-strewn frock. The Collies from the Estelle Blake Collective, for whom Nelis had worked for years, turned up en masse in their corporate blacks, although they *had* pinned gardenias to their lapels.

Jacaranda Fairling was there, almost unrecognisable in yellow instead of purple, and her assistant, Lucida, wore a fabulous creation of embroidered flowers. Her husband, a quiet elf man who looked like Asher, held her hand gently throughout, as if fearing she might drift away.

Nelis said *I do* with a vigour that startled the celebrant, and Frances and Niall's Evangeline made a beeline for the lilypond before Flick and Chas's George intercepted her.

The wedding was chaotic and perfect.

Lucy Tan, having made it to the Gardens apparently by sheer force of determination, hugged Nelis and Xavier after the presentation. Her green, flower-garlanded Queen of the May dress, a gift from her friend Lorelei Herron, hung in graceful folds, giving her the appearance of a small, dynamic galleon under sail.

"I won't be able to stay for supper," she confided. "Deq's going to take us back to the gate. Mistress Joan will let me through, and Jack Miller and Gran Qin will see me back to Paris."

"Thanks for coming, darling Lucy," Nelis said. "But really, I told you that you didn't need platform shoes."

"And I told *you* I didn't want to be trotting about on level with your boobs." She patted her bump. "Luckily, Mayflower will be much taller than I am. Paris is tall."

Paris was indeed tall, as Nelis had noted when she met him a few days before the wedding. He presented as a typical water-lad with long limbs, beautiful skin, and hair that could dry with a single shake, but he also looked like his human father. He even sometimes wore clothes, which was rare in water-folk. He couldn't come to the wedding, but his dad, Jack, had attended as his proxy to make sure Lucy made it safely home.

"How's Dequan?" Nelis asked.

In the weeks since her Christmas wish she had wondered off and on about Lucy's cousin, but she had been too busy to make any detailed enquiries. Besides, she was unwilling to tell Lucy about the wish in case nothing came of it.

She trusted Flick Dark, but after all, this was the human realm.

Lucy's eyes lit up. "Oh, Nel—he's *wonderful.* I've never seen him so happy, and I can't tell you how relieved I am."

"He's found Tamzin Herrick?" She'd semi-expected it, but still . . .

Lucy looked perplexed. "No—why would you think that?"

"Well, you seemed to think that's what he needed to be happy. To get closure."

"Never mind closure . . . he met *the* most perfect woman when he went for his mystery holiday. Her name's Martina Bless, and she's beautiful. Nothing like his other girlfriends, but then, none of them was ever like any of the others, except they were all stunning. They came up here for a week to meet everyone, but Deq's moving down to Patterdale to be with her, because his business is much easier to shift than hers. That's why they're here now—to sort out his stuff." She looked sad for a moment. "It means an end to our spag tom lunches and suppers when I come off the island, but then I'll hardly have time once Mayflower is born. Speaking of whom, I've had a backache for the past two hours, and I've just realised it isn't constant. It's coming in sort of waves . . ." She clutched Nelis' hands and swayed forward to kiss her. "Nel, I've got to go. Xav, will you yell out for Jack? Tell him it's show time!"

Xavier obligingly found Jack Miller, who sent a text to Dequan and took charge of his daughter-in-law with fatherly affection and not the slightest sign of panic. Jack was married to a water maid, so presumably he enjoyed the unexpected.

After they'd gone, Xavier returned to Nelis. "Greet you, Mistress Partridge."

"Goodness, so I am. I'm glad we didn't choose to hyphenate, or we'd be Mister and Missus Winter-Partridge like something out of a children's wildlife documentary."

"It's time to cut the cake," he said.

It wasn't, quite, but they cut it eventually and everyone feasted on Nelis' favourite marmalade sponge made by Xavier's mother and a tribe of aunts.

Nelis reflected that life couldn't be better. Pity her wish hadn't worked, but she would never tell Flick. Dequan Qin had sorted himself out, and that was the main thing.

Took him long enough.

The thought came unbidden and gave her a tiny chill.

Don't be so uncharitable, Nelis Comice Winter Partridge. It's taken you nearly as long, but you got there in the end.

Someone put his arms around her from behind and kissed her neck.

Nelis felt her insides dissolve.

She wondered if there was a nook somewhere so she could have Xavier in her wedding dress . . ."Xav, can you cast a glamour?"

The world went quiet.

Part Seven: Tamzin

Chapter Nineteen: Music

Tamzin, Delphinium Island, March, 2021

M usic Alexandra Delphinium Campania was born in March, close to the birthday Tamzin still celebrated as hers. Matin said he saw no reason why she shouldn't have two — an official Queen's Birthday on March the first along with her private one in January.

Music arrived after a hard, fast labour, during which Matin set Tamzin's prepared recording of *Lullabies for Music* to play softly in the background.

Tamzin thought it was debatable that anyone heard it over her yells, but Eve Adeste, their serene midwife, said yelling was fine, as it released tension. She'd brought along her man, Raph, whom she said was excellent with fathers, but he wasn't really needed. Matin was used to Tamzin yelling, after all.

After Music was bathed and snuggled against Tamzin's chest, she promptly went to sleep.

Eve kissed them all before she and Raph went to get some dinner. Eve was staying on the island for a couple of days in case anyone needed help.

No one did.

Tamzin felt tired, and sore, but oddly invigorated. She thought maybe staying awake so much during the Hot had trained her body to exist with little sleep.

She looked down at their daughter. "She has ears like yours."

"And fingers like yours," Matin said, gently opening the child's small hand.

"Why isn't she all squished and bruisy?"

"Why would she be?"

"Babies are."

"Was Florence? Or Daffodil? Or Dickon?"

"No-o. But I didn't see them on the first day."

"They probably weren't, and neither is Music." Matin sighed, sounding utterly contented. "Music is such a perfect name for her."

"Even though our plan of having her born to a gentle lullaby didn't exactly work."

"It was playing in the background."

"And I was hollering in the foreground." Tamzin smiled. "It hurt. A lot."

"Life does hurt, sometimes."

"Yes, but it's like the apple tree. Remember what you said when you gave me my dolphin pendant?"

"Beautiful things are never really lost."

"Okay, maybe it's not so apposite after all." She shifted to a more comfortable position. "I wonder if Kelp has been born yet."

"I have no idea." He added, "I'm glad you gave up the idea of having Music in the sea."

"Ye-es. Eve said it would be better for her to be born in her home. I was born in a taxi."

"I know."

"Bloody typical. No fixed address even then."

"You have one now."

"Yes. Wherever you are. Speaking of which, I wonder where *they* are."

Matin said, "They know where *you* are, and they knew about Music, so who knows—they might come to call one day."

"Or send that very odd delivery driver with a copy of their latest book."

"That book!" Matin laughed.

"I've remembered where I saw her before — the driver, I mean. It was at the dog park. I should have realised before, because she the little harlequin dog with her, both times. At the park, she was posing as Animal Control."

"Why?" Matin asked.

"I have no idea. Wait — maybe she acts as driver to dogs."

Music stirred, closing her fist around Matin's finger.

Eve put her head in. "All right, lovies?"

"Yes. Did you have a good dinner?"

"We did. We brought you some soup. Raph?"

Her man came in bearing a tray. He beamed at them as Eve took Music and laid her in a cradle. It was beautifully carved from apple wood by the same sculptor who had made the statues at the Fairy Gardens. Tamzin loved it, and she loved Matin even more for arranging it.

Tamzin sipped the soup. It tasted hauntingly familiar. "This is just like the broth Andy gave me when I was landsick on Summer Island. It was his cousin's recipe."

Raph said, "I made this batch. My grandma's recipe."

"Is she fay?"

"Not as far as I know."

"Recipes get shared through the gates," Eve said.

"Like music. It's just what I needed."

Eve said, "We'll take the bowls to wash, and we'll also feed the dogs and Hush. Then, Raph will go back to Sydney to deal with Rasputin. If he feels undervalued, he claws the soft furnishings. I'll stay here for as long as you need me."

Tamzin gave her a grateful look. "I suppose Doctor Lorelei had her baby?"

"Yes, last month. A little lad."

"What did they call him?"

Raph said, "A rather odd name, actually."

"Not Atapeke?"

"That's it. Atapeke Ferris Herron. How did you know?"

Tamzin closed her eyes.

Bleddy hell! My doctor named her son after my dog's son.

"All went well. After all, he is their third child," Eve said.

Tamzin recovered quickly from the birth. When Music was a week old, she and Matin took her through the cliff gate to meet Mariner and Meri. Meri had her baby bound to her chest in a soft sling, but she untied him to display.

Mariner said, "When your sprog gets a few months, we'll give her seagift, so she can swim with us."

"You too," Meri assured them. "This one has it already." She laid her baby in the swell, and he cooed, buoyed by the waves.

"Do you think that will be safe?" Tamzin asked when they returned to Delphinium House.

"I should think so. Mariner's pride would never let him allow harm to come to anyone in his care."

"Maybe we can invite Misty to bring Florence, too. Can you get me my drawing things?"

"What an idle maid you are."

"No fair. I'm feeding Music and there's a pony on my foot and two dogs and a teddy bear against my knees."

Matin handed her a book, and she drew one-handedly while supporting her suckling baby in the other arm.

"What's that—a fish?"

"No, it's Kelp. Emily wanted a water child for the next Jacaranda Journey book."

"I thought it was a trilogy."

"So did we, but Emily says there's still more story to tell."

"Emily is right," Matin said, and Tamzin thought he wasn't talking about the Jacaranda Journey books.

CHAPTER TWENTY: GIFTS

Tamzin, Patterdale, April, 2021

In April, Tamzin went to the Counterpoint Festival in Patterdale. Courtesan were playing, albeit only three sets, since both halves of the duo now had children.

Jordana and Chess's son Joss was happy in his father's arms while his mother sang, but Tansy and Court's little daughter was inclined to be noisy. Indeed, they seemed perplexed that they'd had a girl at all.

Jordy said vaguely that Court had said once too often that his father's family generally had only one child, and that was always a boy, whereupon, she added, Tansy had threatened to twist his nether whiskers.

"She's usually a lovely girl, but just now and again she gets an attack of the potty mouth," she said, shaking her head. "So, Eager Elf? All well? Care to play a guest spot with us while Court wrangles Cathy?"

"Perfect and of course," Tamzin said.

She glanced over to Nell's van, where Matin sat cuddling Music. He had manfully said nothing when she announced her intension of going to Counterpoint, but she'd seen the worry in his face, and casually asked if he'd care to come too. Aunt Mim and Costas had gone to the island to *hold down the fort*, as Costas put it, and Tamzin knew they'd do a fine job. She entertained herself by wondering what would happen if they chanced to go through the cliff gate for a bit of alfresco *tally-ho*. It was quite likely, because Costas had an affinity with the fay goats as well as with Mim. He and Nanny Lutana enjoyed long conversations in the strange dialect Costas referred to as *bleat talk*. Tamzin had no idea what that was all about.

Maybe we should have warned them about Mariner and Meri.

Or maybe not. She thought Costas would be the equal of any seaman ever born. The idea of them slinging insults was rather enjoyable. Nanny might referee.

Like Winterwatch at Dancing Creek, Music at Macquarie, and Oakengrove at Fiddle Bay, Patterdale's Counterpoint festival was short on accommodation for visitors. Obviously, it wasn't viable for providers to build more infrastructure for events that were annual, because it would leave them functionally idle for most of the year. That was why Delphinium Island planned four major *Arts in Tune* festivals a year, each focused on a different branch of the arts, plus smaller workshops.

Their inaugural festival was to be in June. That one would focus on musical instruments slightly to the left of the field, and Tamzin hoped Courtesan would agree to take part, since lutists weren't common.

She also had hopes of the young band known as 4Ts-Quad, whose members played several instruments including a bodhran, a sweetwood flute, and an odd combination of drum and strings called a woodlin.

She had indulged her fancy for a new dress from *Fairings*, beautifully simple in white with a silver embroidered belt especially for the launch of *Winter Arts in Tune*.

For accommodation at Counterpoint, she and Matin had made do with his old van, which he'd bought from Terry Wilde when he bought the recording equipment. They had a makeshift bed in the back, along with Music's cradle. It was cramped, so rather than retire as soon as the last set played, they took Music and went for a walk through the festival venues with Nell and Pepe.

"*Fee Kaffee* is still open," Nell said, indicating a brightly lit sign.

"Let's go and see if they can give us some dinner," Tamzin suggested. "Otherwise, we can go to the *Pride of Erin*."

"*Fee Kaffee*," Nell said. "Pubs are too noisy, and that publican always seems to see a little too much."

"Really?"

A shadow crossed Nell's pleasant face and she glanced down at Pepe.

They strolled over the street and entered the open-air garden. There was a table free, so they settled down.

Music woke and Matin handed her to Tamzin to be fed. She'd had her elf costume modified a little by making an opening in the jerkin. She unclipped the flap and her daughter hungrily attached herself.

"What are you staring at?" Tamzin asked her husband.

"I expect he's wondering if he'll ever get a chance to enjoy a bit of face time again," Nell said absently.

"*What?*"

"Face time. That's what Brian and I call it. Maybe you say something different."

"Oh."

"Judging from your expressions, that's not being a problem to you," Nell said. "Forget I spoke."

Tamzin giggled, surprising herself. It was good to be at a festival again, and good to be with Nell. Of all her friends, Nell was the one who was the least work. It came to her that they had never had the faintest hint of a disagreement, and there was no interpretation required. Nell always said exactly what she meant, and it was always kindly intended. Nell was one of her circle — one of her chosen family.

She ducked her face to kiss her daughter's downy head.

"Hello, have you had a chance to look at the menu yet?" a pleasant voice asked.

Nell said, "We haven't, but do you have any of that *eierbrot* your baker makes? And maybe soup?"

"Certainly. It's chicken and barley today, and we have complementary *alpenkuchen* or apricot strudel. Yannick got distracted and went overboard with the puddings."

"I'll have that, then, with the strudel. Elfie? Matin?"

"Sounds good to me," Matin said. "Tamzin, do you want that too?"

"Mm . . . yum. Maybe some of that crumbly cheese and some figs and walnuts too, I'm hungry."

There was a sudden disconcerted pause, and Tamzin looked up at the waiter.

His hair was sun-bleached brown, and he had a wide, dependable face with something vaguely oriental about the set of his eyes. It was a nice face, and she smiled.

He went on staring.

Has he never seen a woman feed her baby before?

She glanced at Matin, to find him looking at her intently. "Yes?"

The waiter put down his note pad. "Tamzin? Tamzin Herrick? *Gott im Himmel*! It *is* you!"

Tamzin's head spun as, yet again, her worlds collided.

She must have moved abruptly, because Music spluttered before seizing the nipple again and continuing to suckle.

Tamzin's mouth tingled, and for a moment she thought she was going lightheaded, but then everything settled back into place with an inaudible click.

Just the way my spy-heeled shoes close.

She smiled. "Hello Dequan! How absolutely wonderful to see you!"

He went on staring.

The tap of heels broke his gaze and he half turned.

Tamzin glanced over to see a woman in a dirndl hurrying towards them. She had her hair up in a milkmaid braid, and her wide, serene face looked troubled.

"*Liebling*?"

Martina Bless, Tamzin thought, recognising the café's owner. She remembered her, and her twin nieces Lili and Chiara, from her earlier visits with Nell.

The woman put her hand on Dequan's shoulder. "Is everything all right, *meine liebe*?"

He nodded, tucking an arm around her. "Yes, *Fräulein*." He blinked a few times, apparently trying to focus.

Martina looked over the table. "I hope nothing's wrong, my friends?"

"Nothing at all," Matin said. Tamzin saw him smile at the woman. "It's just that my wife and your—" He left it hanging.

"Dequan and I are betrothed," she said.

"My wife and your betrothed used to know one another. I think they were both a bit taken aback to meet so unexpectedly."

Martina's smiling gaze swept over the table. "I see this is a cause for celebration. I'll have the twins take over the serving and you can have time to catch up." She turned to Dequan. "This will be your Tamzin you lost so long ago?"

He nodded, looked confused, and shook his head.

Tamzin said, "We knew one another a long time ago, and I left without saying goodbye. I couldn't help it—at least, I thought I couldn't."

"You can talk about it now. First, I'll take your order."

Nell repeated the order, even remembering the nuts and figs for Tamzin, and Martina swung an extra chair over to the table.

Dequan sat down, still in his server's apron. He rubbed his hand through his hair. "Tamzin, I'm really not sure what to say!"

"Would you like us to go to another table?" Nell asked Tamzin. "Pepe and me, I mean."

"No, it's fine. Just one thing—I should have asked before.

Nell, have you ever had disclosure?"

Nell said slowly, "If you mean did I know your husband is some variety of fay, yes, I did know. Years ago, before I met Dean, my first husband, I went out a few times with a pixie lad. It wasn't serious—I was friendly with his sister. They gave me a few pointers on how to pick your people, Matin. And of course, there are some of the Dames—" She broke off. "You'll know who I mean, I reckon. Pud, for instance." She looked at Dequan. "You?"

He said, "A wee bit of courtfolk. Not enough to mention. Martina's alpenfee. So are the twins, and Yannick the baker."

"I gathered that. Martina doesn't exactly hide it, and the mädchens are like her. That is the right term?"

"It is." He smiled. "I call her *fräulein,* but that's just a nick-name. She's a dream I had—a dream come true."

Nell continued to Tamzin, "So, how is disclosure relevant to how you know Dequan, Elfie?"

Dequan said, "We were at school together for a couple of years, back in Sydney."

Matin said, mildly, "You can say what you like in front of me. I know Tamzin loved you for a very long time. I'm fortunate that she came to love me more."

Dequan nodded, and Tamzin saw him relax. "Same story with me and Martina, I suppose. I met her just four months ago, and I can't imagine how I ever managed to be *me* without her. We're going to be married next month."

Tamzin said, "I first saw Matin the night I last saw you, but we didn't get together as a couple until much later."

"And now you have a baby."

"Her name's Music," Matin said.

"Music Alexandra Delphinium Campania," Tamzin supplied. It still gave her a thrill to speak the beautiful name they had chosen.

Dequan said, "I like that. It sings. My cousin Lucy—

remember her? She has a baby girl called Mayflower Valentine. Nothing to do with pilgrim fathers. Everything to do with flowering hawthorn and the day she was born. She's just a bit older than your Music, I should think."

Tamzin said, "I'd better tell you right away that I know Annie Blue. She didn't know who I was to you when we met and I'm not sure she does even now. Just in case you thought I'd been stalking you."

"Annie —" His face cleared. "Oh, you mean Stace Blugle! How is she?"

"Very well. I handle the artwork for her advertising campaigns." She saw he didn't understand, and so added, "She's a fitness coach. The latest program is called *Electric Annie*."

"So, you kept on with your painting and went commercial?"

"Tamzin runs Elf-Made Art, commercial *and* high end," Nell said.

Dequan turned an amazed face to her. "I've seen some of that . . . a painting yay high of a little yorkie, done of a medallion — right?" He held his finger and thumb apart. "Liv Bellover wears it and shows it off to anyone she can. Remember her, Tam? She was at school with Lucy."

Tamzin shook her head. "I mean, I did a court portrait for her, but I don't know her otherwise."

"Okay, maybe she didn't start at Diversity High until you'd left. Come to that, we both left at the same time. She and Lucy-Lou weren't friends, exactly. They were both up for the lead in one of the musicals — I'm sorry. I'm babbling." He sounded uncertain.

Tamzin said, "I think I'd better tell you what happened after the formal."

He nodded. "I'd like to know, if it's all right —"

"I know already," Matin said. "Tamzin, I think Music's gone to sleep."

"Oh . . ."

"I'll take her." He put out his arms and Tamzin unhooked her daughter and passed her across, tugging her jerkin into place as she did so.

Nell said, "Do you need a napkin, Elfie?"

"Thanks." Tamzin stuffed the napkin in her top. Then she turned her attention to Dequan and began.

"Do you remember how angry my parents were when they caught us kissing?"

"I should say so."

"I expect it seemed an extreme reaction to you, because we did have our clothes on, and we were nearly eighteen—well, we thought I was. The thing is, they hadn't realised how close we were. They had no idea we had plans for after Christmas. I'd never told them because I was out of the habit of telling them *anything* in case they used it against me. No—that's unfair. They wouldn't have done it to spite me—they'd have done it *in spite* of what I wanted, so I felt better that they didn't know."

"You always kept your cards close to your chest," Dequan said. "It was only after you disappeared that I realised how little I really knew about you."

Tamzin told her long story, sitting there in the café garden with her husband and her baby, her reliable friend, an old chihuahua, and her first love. There were breaks when Martina's look-alike nieces, who introduced themselves as Lili and Chiara Langel-Bless, served their order, and when Martina and a dark young man who reminded them he was Yannick the baker came to see if they needed anything more.

Tamzin had the feeling they all wanted a good look at Dequan's first love.

Dequan asked if Martina cared to sit down with them, but she shook her head, saying she had patrons to see to. "You can tell me later, *liebling*, if that's all right?" She glanced at

Tamzin.

"Yes, that's fine. It's his story too, in a way."

Martina went away and Tamzin continued. "I came back through the gateway at the tor in July that year, the day before Winterwatch started."

Dequan said, "Was that two-thousand-and-seventeen?"

She nodded.

"I was there! Stace and I went for the weekend. We drove up early on the Saturday."

"So, we just missed one another."

"It wasn't really Stace's thing, but she tried, bless her. I was always fond of Stace."

"So are Matin and I," Tamzin said. "She came to our wedding."

"We split a few months after Winterwatch—her choice."

That wasn't quite the way Annie had told it, but Tamzin let it go.

"I must have met Delphine soon after, then Puck . . ."

Tamzin almost said something tart about serial monogamy, but she remembered, just in time, that she'd told him about Cornelius and Shay, Arne, Bayeux, and Andy, although not in great detail.

"I caught the bus, then took the train down to the city to see Branok St Ives. He's my solicitor and a good friend—more or less my surrogate father. Matin recommended him, but it took me a long time to follow it up. I stayed with him and his wife for a few weeks while he helped me to get my life in order. After that—" She broke off.

Matin said, "You might as well tell him, sweetheart."

Nell gave her a sharp look. "Have we come to the day *we* met?"

"Yes—though, actually, I think I first saw you at Winterwatch."

"You might have—wait, was I wearing my orange skirt?"

"Yes, and you had Pepe."

"I always have Pepe." Nell looked down affectionately at her elderly chihuahua and slipped him a piece of Tamzin's cheese.

Dequan's face creased into a grin. "I remember that skirt. Stace thought it was *radical*. In a good way. Stace always thinks of things in a good way."

Tamzin said, "Branok had given me your address, and I caught the ferry to Milson's Point and walked over to Gilchrist to see you. I saw Lucy — she didn't see me — and because I wanted to talk to you in private, I went back to get a coffee at *Paws a While*. Then I went to your place and saw you come out with Annie. You were going for a run. I didn't know her then, but I could see you were a couple, so I went back to the café — "

"Where she put on a brave face and had coffee with me and some of the other Dames with Dogs, and sketched portraits of dogs on napkins," Nell put in.

" . . . making friends for life, and incidentally, beginning the *sunshine* part of my business."

Dequan shook his head. "I didn't see you. If I had — "

"You'd have said hello."

"Yes, of course! I'd have been — Why didn't you say anything?"

"I realised I had no right to disrupt your life. And yes, I see now I made a great drama out of bricks with no straw. Why should I think *I* had the power to disrupt you? As a very annoying person I know says, *water under the bridge*.

"Anyway, I left. I went back to Bran and Gill's, and soon after, I moved up to Fiddle Bay, and started Elf-Made Art officially. I was working on a super-life-sized portrait of my friend Daylight and her friend — her husband now — when I met Matin again. That was in November of two thousand and eighteen.

"In March the next year, Annie came to me as a client. It was a shock, because I recognised her as your girlfriend. She's memorable, but of course, she didn't know me."

"She's one of a kind, all right." He gave an affectionate smile. "I'm surprised she didn't know you, though. I have photos of you that Augie Herron took on the night of our formal on my life-board."

Tamzin bit her lip. Had Annie always known?

"People don't always look closely at things they see every day," Matin said quietly.

"No. I guess not. And I suppose Stace never really paid attention to that sort of thing. She was never the jealous kind, and she never looks back."

"I gathered she'd broken up with you, but—"

Matin said, "I suggested Tamzin might go to you then, but, to my eternal gratitude, she decided to stay with me."

Dequan said, "She was always daft about elves. Figures she would marry one."

Matin continued, "We were married in June last year, and we moved to Delphinium Island to start *Arts in Tune*. Music was born last month.

"Tamzin has been going around the festival circuit with Nell since she came back from the tor, and this time I decided to come with her."

"And that brings my story up to date," Tamzin said.

"I guess it also explains why I could never trace your family after you disappeared. The people I was enquiring about didn't really exist."

"I hope you didn't waste too much time trying," she said, remembering Emily.

"I won't pretend I've been searching for the past decade— well, obviously I haven't, since you've been back in plain sight for so long. The practice I got into back then when I *was* searching did give me a job though—I trade as Qin-Find. I trace hard-to-source information and items, and mostly, I find them."

"I know. Branok told me."

"But how odd. We obviously know some of the same people. It's strange that no one told me they'd seen you. Jezz Finchley, for instance. I see her now and again — well I did, up until I moved down here. I source vintage printed cloth for her."

"I haven't been in contact with Jezz since I came back. I'd love to see her again, but so far I haven't made the effort."

"Finchley Design — she's done all right, our Jezz. I'm sure she'd like to catch up with you again." He pondered for a moment and then went on. "Lucy . . . it's not so odd you haven't been talking to her, since she spends so much time on Ferris Island or off the radar with her man, but — oh, there are lots of people we both know who might have seen you."

"Such as who?"

"Well — Nelis Winter. She's that friend of Lucy's who married Xavier Partridge a few weeks ago. Or Otto — he used to have a thing for Lucy. Even Augie Herron's still around at Diversity High, and he'd remember us both."

"Otto would be Otto Fairling?" Matin asked.

"Yes. You know him?"

"We do. Matin worked with him for years, but we haven't seen him in a while, other than at our wedding." Tamzin said.

"Who *have* you seen that you knew before?"

"Hmm . . . not Mister Herron, but his wife, Lorelei is my doctor. I'd never met her before she was recommended to me, though, and I doubt if she knows Tamzin Campania was ever in her husband's art class. I've seen Otto's mother, who owns the shop where I got my wedding dress — and the dress I wore to our formal. Mind you, I didn't know she was Otto's mother the first time around. I didn't even know there *was* an Otto, then."

"How about the artist you met at the Twenty-Twenty Exhibition?" Matin asked.

"Jack Miller! Oh, of course! He remembered me. He was the groundsman at Diversity High. Did you know he's an illustrator?"

"Yes, so it happens—and here's a coincidence. He's Lucy Lou's father-in-law . . . more or less."

"He said his wife and son couldn't come to the exhibition," Tamzin said. She frowned slightly, remembering what else Jack had said, or maybe *not* said. He'd certainly mentioned Lucy—and Dequan, but he'd *never* suggested Lucy was any more to him than a past pupil at the school where he worked.

"No—they're waterfolk," Dequan said.

"Oh." She put the thought away. Mister Miller, who was also Jonathan Blarney, was under no obligation to tell her his son was in love with her old love's cousin.

She took a deep breath. "I talked to him for quite a while, but he didn't say you were looking for me."

"He wouldn't know that," Dequan said. "I went to Augie Herron early in two-thousand-and-ten, but I didn't ask anyone else at the school. What was the point? We'd both left, and Augie would have known where you were, if anyone did." He bit his thumb in the way Tamzin suddenly remembered. "It looks as if we've been skirting around one another for the past three years. The people who know us both have no reason to mention us to one another."

He was silent for a while, and Tamzin watched the various emotions play over his face. He had always been expressive.

"You know where I am now," she ventured. "We live on Delphinium Island, and we have contact details on our websites." She fished cards out of the pocket of her costume.

He gave a quick smile. "I do. I'm glad about that." He looked down at the business cards. "The thing is, I have no idea how else to feel about it. I've been trying to think, how would I have felt if I'd met you last year, say, or even two or three years ago. I think I'd have been pleased—more than pleased."

"Not angry?"

"I never was angry, but I won't pretend it was easy. I always thought your parents must have wanted to get you away from me very badly, but I could never work out why. I had a few ideas, but none of them made sense. I mean, they couldn't *really* have minded that half my family come from gold rush immigrant stock and that I'm a trace fay. Why would they? How would they even know, unless you'd told them?"

Tamzin said, "They didn't know, and they wouldn't have cared—although they definitely hated it when I painted elves. If it helps, it wasn't personal. They did the same thing with my best friend when I was eleven or so. It was about me getting too close to *anyone*. They didn't do long-term friendships, and they didn't see why I should, either."

Dequan said, "That does help, I think. But you know, I'm glad we met *now* rather than last year."

"Why's that?"

"Well, because I have Martina—she's mine in the way no one else ever was or could be—not even you. And last year you already had Matin. And you'd already made your choice. I wouldn't have—I mean, I *hope* I'd have been civilised about it, but I'm glad I wasn't tested." He turned his attention to Matin. "Has it occurred to you that we look a wee bit alike?"

"Yes, as soon as I saw your portrait in Tamzin's collection," Matin said bluntly. "Our Tamzin evidently likes tall men with messy brown hair and hazel eyes with a slight tilt to them."

"I *am* here, you know," Tamzin said.

"On the other hand, this meeting has shot down one of my other theories," Matin said to Tamzin.

"What?"

"Do you remember when I said you and Annie would obviously be friends because you were both attracted to the same sort of man?"

"Yes. She loved Dequan and she fancied you, but she got over it when we were betrothed. What's your point, Master Campania?"

"Meeting Mistress Bless has shot that theory down. You, Annie, and she are totally different types, physically speaking."

"So we are. What have your other girlfriends looked like, Dequan?"

Dequan said, "Well, you know Jezz. I went about with her for a bit, but it was never serious. We're still friends. Puck is as tall as I am, and fair and elegant. Delphine is short and dark and intense."

"Okay. We've established you don't have a particular type, but Annie and I do. The plus one date she brought to our wedding had brown hair . . . what was his name, Matin?"

"Plus one," Matin said unhelpfully.

"Anyway, he was a tallish brown-haired plus one and they looked cosy."

Nell said, with interest, "My husbands looked a bit alike, and the pixie lad I was seeing was the same general type. The blokey sort that look good in jeans. And Brian first fancied me because I was having a wardrobe malfunction that reminded him of his first wife. Someone ought to write a treatise."

"I expect someone has," Matin said.

Tamzin looked from one to the other. *"Bleddy hell!"* She thought briefly of Shay and Cornelius, Arne, Bayeux and Andy, a redhead, three blonds and a brunet. She'd left them all and the only one she might have considered staying with was Andy . . . the darkest and least polished of the blonds— who had messy hair.

Martina came over to their table at that point, calm and

smiling. "Is there anything else I can offer you?"

"No thanks," Tamzin said. It occurred to her that she and Dequan had chosen forevers with similar names, but she wasn't saying that. It would set Nell off again.

Matin said, "It's probably time we turned in. Music will be awake again by one in the morning. I'll take her to the van, Tamzin, if you want to stay here a while and talk old times."

"No, I'll come with you."

"And talk new times," Martina said.

"Well—yes."

"There is one more thing to do, though. Remember what we agreed?" Matin nodded down towards Tamzin's feet. "Your shoe, Mistress Campania."

"Oh yes—"

"What's this then? Cinderella revisited?" Dequan asked.

"No. Reallio, trulio—"

"Daggers and toes," he said, grinning.

"You remembered!"

"Ogden Nash? God, *schat,* who could forget?"

Nell cleared her throat. "What's this about shoes? Mind you, I've always thought that pair was a bit special. I think of them as your Dorothy shoes. Do you ever click them to go home?"

"I *am* home," Tamzin said. She blew a kiss to Matin. Then, she pushed her chair back and she bent to remove her spy-heeled sandal. It had guarded its secret for long enough.

Not that it was much of a secret. Matin knew exactly what was in there.

She swivelled the heel aside and removed the small parcel wrapped in galleonfee cloth. She weighed it in her hand for the last time.

"I've imagined this moment so often," she said.

Martina suddenly held up her hand. "Wait—*liebling,* you have something in your cabinet for your Tamzin. Would you like to have it now to give to her?"

Dequan said, "Yes, *Fräulein*. It's time, I think!" The alpenfee put one hand on his shoulder and he put up his hand to cover it.

The gesture was one of unstudied affection, and Tamzin was glad. Martina Bless was nothing like her, and she was perfect for Dequan.

The woman's other hand moved, and she was suddenly holding a small cloth pouch. She handed it to Dequan and stood back.

Dequan held up the bag. "Do you remember when I said I had a gift for you that Christmas? I was going to give it to you *over there,* in a beautiful place."

"I remember. And *I* said I had something for you, too — but I didn't right then. What I had was an intention to get you something special. Even when I was dragged away, I was still sure I'd get that gift to you somehow.

"I did find something. While I was *over there,* if you remember, I spent rather too much time on a very strange island, Stella Orris. It's the central island in an archipelago they call the Star Pin."

"I've heard of that," Martina said. She sounded interested. "It's a place that gives the sight to those who don't have it. Or so they say."

"I'm not sure that it gave *me* the sight, but I found something special, and I also lost something that was special to me then. I spent a lot of time drawing all the people I remembered knowing." She looked steadily at Dequan. "I left you until last because you were the most important to me then. Only I ran out of paper, so I drew your portrait on the sand, and the tide washed it away."

Martina, she noted from the corner of her eye, made a sudden *aha* movement with her hand, as if something made sense to her. Maybe it did.

"What did you lose?" the alpenfee asked.

Tamzin said, "Dequan, do you remember at our formal, you gave me a rose? A very small, perfect one."

"Elf Maid. The plant is still growing in Mum's garden. It flowers every year. I had some cuttings from it in pots back in Gilchrist . . ."

"That's it. After I went to Macquarie Bay, I dipped it in resin, to preserve it. While I was *over there*, I wore it as a pendant, oh, for years! Then, on Stella Orris, I lost it somehow. I know where it is, because someone found it later, but it was out of my reach. I started wearing the gift I found for you in its place. I went on wearing that until I met Matin again . . ."

"And I asked her if she'd mind removing it when we were together," Matin said.

"I did that, but I didn't want to lose it, so I hid it in my shoe. And, as Matin just reminded me—"

"I see you have another necklace now," Martina remarked.

Tamzin stroked her wooden dolphin. "Yes, and I'll wear this one forever."

She held out the cloth-wrapped package. "I don't expect you'll want to wear this, but I know you have, or used to have, a collection of odd things. You might put this in with those."

Dequan reached out, and she dropped the package into his palm.

He unwrapped it, and lifted out the orris stone disc. He held it up between finger and thumb. "This is interesting. Do you know what it is?"

"I call it orris stone. It's the only piece I found."

"Thank you. It's a good deal prettier than most of my curios. Especially the goose feather pin." He exchanged a long, significant look with Martina, who, unexpectedly, blushed.

"Look through it," Tamzin said. She was curious to see what, if anything, he might see.

Dequan lifted the disc to his left eye and closed the other

one.

"Oh!" He sounded startled.

"What is it?" Martina asked.

"Not what—where. I think I'm seeing into somewhere else." He handed it to her.

Martina raised it to her eye. *"Grus Gott im Himmel!"*

Dequan said, "Martina has *the sight*."

"A lot of alpenfee have," Martina said. She went on looking through the stone. "This is a wonder!"

"Are you sure you want to part with it?" Dequan asked. "You might give it to Matin or keep it for your daughter."

"It was meant for you," Tamzin said.

Matin said, quietly, "I have something far more precious, and Music will have a keepsake from the Bellflower chest."

"I see, and I'll accept it happily," Dequan said. He handed the small bag to Tamzin. "This was always meant for you. It's created, not natural, but it's the only one. A halfling pisky jeweller made it for me."

Tamzin glanced at Martina, who smiled back. "You'll like this, my dear . . . I think it's pretty but, as your man said, I have something far more precious, and this was meant for you."

Tamzin said, "I have friends who are piskies."

"This one is called Tane Pendennis."

"Believe it or not—"

"You know him?"

"No, not at all, but my friend Branok is related to the Pendennis family at a place called Treborrow. Some of them are muties, if you know what I mean."

"Tane is from that family," Dequan said. "He goes around the markets, which I find odd. He's a water halfling, like Lucy-Lou's Paris, but Paris couldn't possibly *pass,* and Tane manages—just."

Tamzin tipped up the bag. A small silver charm fell into

her hand. She held it up, smiling with relief. "It's lovely . . . look, Matin! It's an elf girl holding a guitar. It's beautifully made." It was. The seventeen-year-old Tamzin Herrick would have adored this piece. It would have been . . . she sought for words.

It would have been validation of myself as a daft elf obsessive who played the guitar.

That's not me now.

Her hand came up to caress her wooden dolphin.

This is me, now, the woman who leaps for joy.

She looked back to Dequan.

And he's not the boy who loved weird things . . . and his schat.

She got up from her chair, went to her first love, and she bent and kissed his cheek. "Thank you, Dequan. It's a lovely charm, and I'll keep it always. I'll show it to Bran, since he's related to the Pendennis line. But of course, the real gift has been seeing you again, and meeting Martina properly."

Matin stood up, holding the sleeping baby against his shoulder, and she turned to him, raising her face.

He kissed her gently, in love and understanding and in a promise which she would redeem, with interest, when she was not quite so sleep-deprived.

She thought longingly of her island, and of Bellflower Cottage. What wouldn't she give . . .

She glanced back at Martina. "Mistress, is there a gateway anywhere round here?"

"Certainly, there is — just a few minutes' drive out of town. My nieces and Yannick go through every night because they live at *Langelhame over there.* If you like to wait one moment, I can get them to show you through. It's time to close anyway."

Tamzin looked appealingly at Matin. "Can we?"

"For you, my dolphin, anything."

"What about the van?"

Dequan said, "You can leave it parked where Yannick parks his and come back to pick it up when you like."

"Oh, *good*. Nell—"

"No worries, loves, though I won't offer to drive your van back to Sydney. I've got mine."

"That's all right. We'll come back tomorrow afternoon in time for the next Courtesan gig."

Martina snapped her fingers. "Girls . . ."

Nell laughed suddenly. "How the other half live! We'd better pay for this dinner."

"Our treat." Matin fished in his pocket with his free hand, gave up, and flicked his hand. "Can I put it on card?"

"*Danke*. Come through . . ."

Matin handed Music to Tamzin.

Nell laughed harder.

"What's so funny?"

Nell spluttered, "Glory be, it just struck me. My friend is married to an elf man, and he *has a credit card*."

Tamzin considered the scene—her husband heading off with her old love's new love to pay for soup and bread, her old love watching his new love with his heart in his eyes, her friend laughing and hugging her darling old dog, her baby sleeping so sweetly . . . her fingers itched to paint them all, but that would have to wait.

ABOUT THE AUTHOR

Lark Westerly loves weaving stories about characters who grow and change while remaining true to themselves. The *Being Tamzin* series has seven books, and the mysteries the characters need to solve were also mysteries for Lark to unpick. Sometimes, that meant moving back to an earlier book to plant a clue. At other times, the clue was there already, put in unintentionally. *So* that's *how it happened! Ah, so* this *is why he said that back then.* Now *I see!* The revelations were great fun for Lark, and she hopes they delight her readers just as much.

Being Tamzin 7 brings the series to a close, so much of it is concerned with closure.

The main questions were answered in the first few chapters, but there were still matters that needed attention. For instance, how would Tamzin finally catch up with Dequan? Fortunately, that fell into place almost by itself in one of those *So* that's *how it happened!* moments. If Music was born in early March, it was possible for Tamzin and Matin to take her to the festival in Patterdale in April. Dequan would be living in Patterdale at that time, having moved down in early January. He would be working part time in his betrothed's café, so why not send Tamzin and her party there for a meal? It could well have been another of those *just missed you* moments, but obviously, it wasn't!

Lark lives on the island of Tasmania, where she is never bored. She has a husband, two adult children, two grandchildren and some dogs. She enjoys walking, reading, photography, generally creating microcosms and researching for whatever she's writing.

For more about Lark and her stories, check out her homepage at https://larksinger.weebly.com

The Being Tamzin companion page, with annotated character lists, terms and places *and* a big spoiler page, is at https://beingtamzin.weebly.com